PENGUI

THE RET

H*Y*M*A*N

A writer of remarkable versatil
United States in 1908. After obtaining a Ph.D. from the Uni-
versity of Chicago he studied at the London School of
Economics. He served in the United States government as
Deputy Director of the Office of War Information, as Special
Consultant to the Secretaries of War and Air and as Consultant
to the Commission on National Goals. He has lectured at Yale
and was Ford Visiting Professor of Political Science at the
University of California. He is a Faculty Associate of Columbia
University and an Honorary Fellow of the London School of
Economics.

Leo Rosten has published books on politics and painting,
sociology and satire, and is a regular contributor to learned
journals. He has written *The Education of H*Y*M*A*N
K*A*P*L*A*N* and the bestselling *The Joys of Yiddish* (1968,
Penguin 1971), a 'relaxed' lexicon of Yiddish, Hebrew and Yin-
glish words encountered in English, combining scholarship with
storytelling. Among his most recent publications are *Hooray for
Yiddish!* and *Leo Rosten's Giant Book of Laughter*. He has also written several film screenplays, including *The Velvet Touch* and
Double Dynamite. He lives in New York, summers at Westhamp-
ton Beach and is a keen traveller in between.

LEO ROSTEN

THE
RETURN
OF
H★Y★M★A★N
K★A★P★L★A★N

PENGUIN BOOKS

To "Mr. Parkhill"
after so many Waterloos

PENGUIN BOOKS

Published by the Penguin Group
27 Wrights Lane, London W8 5TZ, England
Viking Penguin Inc., 40 West 23rd Street, New York, New York 10010, USA
Penguin Books Australia Ltd, Ringwood, Victoria, Australia
Penguin Books Canada Ltd, 2801 John Street, Markham, Ontario, Canada L3R 1B4
Penguin Books (NZ) Ltd, 182–190 Wairau Road, Auckland 10, New Zealand

Penguin Books Ltd, Registered Offices: Harmondsworth, Middlesex, England

First published 1959
Published in Penguin Books 1968
This revised edition first published in Great Britain, in a volume entitled
O K*A*P*L*A*N! My K*A*P*L*A*N!, by Constable and Co. 1979
Published in Penguin Books 1988

1 3 5 7 9 10 8 6 4 2

Made and printed in Great Britain by
Richard Clay Ltd, Bungay, Suffolk

CONTENTS

WARNING

The God-fearing characters in these tales do not portray persons living, dormant or dead.

Readers who insist that Miss Mitnick or Mr. Hruska, Olga Tarnova or Casimir Scymczak, act exactly like the neighbor upstairs are hallucinating: The people in these stories *do* live upstairs, but only in the house of my imagination.

L. R.

1

THE PRODIGAL S·O·N

"Miss Mary Atrakian."

"Yes, sor."

"Olaf Umea."

"In place!"

"Mr. Stanislaus—uh—Wilkomirski."

"I am."

"Mrs. Minnie Pilpul."

"Likevise."

Mr. Parkhill did not call the roll in alphabetical order because he was trying to familiarize himself with the new faces, matching each face to a name in the order in which the members of the class had selected their seats.

"Miss Lola Lopez."

"Sí!"

"Mr. Vasil—Hruska? Is that right? The 'H,' I take it, is silent. . . ."

Mr. Hruska was silent, too. In fact, there was no Mr. Hruska. "My name is Olansky!" protested the burly man with very thick glasses at whom Mr. Parkhill was smiling. "Reuben Olansky."

"Oh, I *beg* your pardon. Where is Mr. Hruska? Mr. H-r-u . . ."

Spelling did not produce Mr. Hruska. Mr. Parkhill put an "X" after the name. A crisp "√" on Mr. Parkhill's attendance sheet signified that the student was present, a reluctant "X" that he or she was not. Sometimes, of course, a student came in well after the class session had begun, in which case Mr. Parkhill simply circled the "X." That meant the student had arrived late. (Miss Schnepfe, in the principal's office, was a stickler about such things. She *hated* tardiness.) "C. J. Fledermann."

"*Ja.*"

"Isaac Nussbaum."

"Here is Isaac Nussbaum."

Mr. Parkhill glanced up. Mr. Nussbaum certainly was there, a little skullcap on his thick hair, a fine, full beard foresting his cheeks and chin. (Mr. Nussbaum was a cantor.)

"Peter Ignatius Studniczka . . ."

Mr. Parkhill tried to call the names cheerfully. But he did not feel cheerful; he felt depressed. It was only the second night of the fall term, and a new term always brought with it fresh promise—new personalities, new problems, new challenges. Yet here and now, a brief forty-eight hours after the season's advent, Mr. Parkhill found himself possessed of melancholy, a melancholy deepened by surprising nostalgia. . . . Last year's names, last year's faces. . . . Ah, that *had* been a beginners' grade. . . .

"Miss Rochelle Goldberg."

"A pleasure." (She amplified the pleasure with a caramel.)

Well, at least some of the old flock had returned.

"Mr. Milas Wodjik."

"Oxcuse, the name is 'Vodjik,' not 'Wodjik'!"

"Oh, thank you." Mr. Parkhill nodded pleasantly. (It was not often that a student corrected a teacher's pronunciation in the American Night Preparatory School for Adults.)

"Mr. Tomas Wodjik."

"Ho huh."

Mr. Parkhill gave Mr. Tomas Wodjik a smile as friendly as the one he had given Mr. Milas Wodjik—but longer scrutiny. He could not tell one Mr. Wodjik from the other. They were twins. They were identical twins. To make things worse, they dressed exactly alike—blue suits, striped shirts, brown knit ties—and sat side by side. (When they had first appeared before Mr. Parkhill, handing him their registration cards, Mr. Parkhill had reached *between* them; he would have to check his glasses.)

"Mr. Lucca Barbella."

"Presente!"

"Miss Kipnis . . ."

"Hello."

"Mr. Nathan P. Nathan?"

"Yes, *sir!* Ready!" came that buoyant laugh.

"Mrs. Yanoff . . ."

"Who alse?"

For some reason, a phrase kept running through Mr. Parkhill's mind: *Où sont les fleurs d'antan?* "Where *were* the Blooms of yesteryear?" Mr. Norman Bloom, rumor had it, had forsaken the temple of learning to toil for a raincoat manufacturer in Passaic, N.J. (What a fierce classroom debater Mr. Bloom had been!) Promotion had advanced the superior scholars—Wolfgang Schmitt, Mr. Finster-wald, Gerta Valuskas, Harry Feigenbaum—to the golden pastures of Miss Higby's Advanced Grammar and Civics. Mr. Jacob Marcus had captured the heart of a comely divorcee and moved, it was said, to a bucolic cottage in Far Rockaway by the sea. Mrs. Tomasic had moved with her husband, Slavko, to Bridgeport. Gus Matsoukas had returned to Greece. Vincente Perez had transferred to a school much closer to his lodgings in the Bronx. Miss Carmen Caravello had gone to Italy "for *piccolo* vacation to see family" (a postcard had informed Miss Mitnick), but

the powerful hold of family, friends and the Mediterranean sun had been too much for Miss Caravello to reject
once more. ("O, I love my madre, padre, sister Angelina
who is in convent," the postcard of Mount Vesuvius erupt-
ing had informed Mr. Parkhill. "Also I am in Love!" Miss
Caravello had sworn never to return to the *"manicomio* of
N.Y.")

And Mr. Kaplan? . . . Mr. Parkhill sighed. He always
sighed when he remembered Mr. Kaplan. No one knew
what had happened to him. Some said he had lost his job,
others that he had lost his voice. Mr. Pinsky believed that
Mr. Kaplan was planning to run for Mayor.

"Mr. Blattberg."

"Good evnink!" A third grandson's baby tooth flashed on
the watch chain Mr. Blattberg proudly twirled.

"Miss Mitnick."

Mr. Parkhill was *very* glad that Miss Mitnick was back.
She was a student any teacher would like—so conscien-
tious, so intelligent, so shy. This wisp of a maiden, offered
richly deserved promotion to Miss Higby's grade, had surrendered to panic, tearfully confessed to not feeling
"ready" for such a dizzying elevation, and pleaded with
Mr. Parkhill to be allowed to remain in his fold for one
more season. So had Nathan P. Nathan. It was a tribute, in
a way. . . .

"Miss Tarnova."

Returned, too, was Olga Tarnova, with her cobalt hair,
her earrings and bracelets, her sultry moans and grand
manner—a faded Cleopatra, floating down a Slavic Nile.
"Da, da." Sometimes, Mr. Parkhill thought Miss Tarnova
could wring tragedy from the multiplication table.

"Mr. Trabish."

Oscar Trabish yawned, as bakers are wont to do.

"Mrs. Moskowitz."

"Oooo." Mrs. Moskowitz had been making heroic efforts
to curb her "Oy!"'s for more Americanized "Ooo"'s.

"Miss Ziev."

Miss Ziev was somewhat subdued. Her marriage to Mr. Andrassy, in Mr. Krout's class, had been delayed by the death of his grandmother. The fact that his grandmother was in Budapest had only lengthened Mr. Andrassy's mourning.

"Mr. Pinsky."

Mr. Pinsky, a little more merry, a little less chubby, was ensconced directly in front of Mr. Parkhill, in the chair in the exact center of the front row. That was where Mr. Kaplan had always roosted. (How could one forget the place from which that intrepid spirit had referred to the Generalissimo of Nationalist China as "Shanghai Jack"?)

Mr. Parkhill put the attendance sheet to one side. "Well, class." He smiled upon them in his most reassuring manner. "Your homework, the first assignment of the semester was—'My Life.'" The first assignment was always "My Life"; the second might be "My Vacation" or "My Job" or "My Ambition"; but the first was always "My Life." Nothing so swiftly enlisted the interest of Mr. Parkhill's novitiates, so rapidly soothed their anxieties and bolstered their morale, as the simple invitation to recount the story of "My Life."

"Miss Lopez, will you please go to the board and transcribe your composition? . . . Mr. Olansky . . . Miss Tarnova . . ." He called off four more names.

They trudged to the blackboards in the single file of the doomed, seven of them: one groaned, two sagged, three sighed, one shuddered. But all advanced to confront their fate. Then they strung themselves along the boards as if deploying for combat. Brows furrowed, lips tightened, papers rustled; then sticks of chalk rose like lances. A few coughs of apology, a few moans of uncertainty, and white letters began to form words that bravely marched across the slate.

Mr. Parkhill strolled down the aisle to the back of the

7

room, as he usually did when the boards were being used. He turned to watch his pilgrims.

Tiny Miss Lopez was standing on tiptoe as she committed her life to the board. Mrs. Yanoff kept wiping her brow as concentration exacted its toll. Olaf Umea muttered. (Every class Mr. Parkhill had ever taught seemed to contain one born mutterer: Gus Matsoukas, who had sought no friends and tendered no confidences, as befitted a Greek among barbarians, had been the mutterer of last year's beginners' grade. Now it was Olaf Umea.) Mr. Oscar Trabish unbuttoned his sleeve to accelerate the circulation in his writing arm. Mr. Reuben Olansky, who seemed to be both far-sighted and near-sighted, kept adjusting his bifocals—the better to stare at his work or glare at Miss Tarnova, on his right. Olga Tarnova . . . her bracelets jangled as she wrote, and she fell into throaty mewings whenever she lifted chalk or pen. From time to time, Miss Tarnova dabbed a lacy handkerchief at her nostrils.

Mr. Parkhill noted how respectful was the silence fallen upon the seated. The tick of the big clock on the wall, stern Washington on one side, sad Lincoln on the other, cast soft punctuations of time in the air. . . . This was a docile class. In *last* year's class, Mr. Parkhill could not help ruminating, chattering or teasings or storm signals would long since have appeared—from Mr. Bloom, as he pounced upon some blunder hatched on the board; or from Miss Valuskas, whose Finnish pencil used to stab upward at the first sign of error; and certainly from Mr. Kaplan as he "t'ought" about some profound point. Mr. Kaplan had always thought out loud—either to consult his private Muses, of whom he had a copious supply, or to grant his colleagues the privilege of participating in his priceless cerebration. (One night, Mr. Kaplan gave the principal parts of "to eat" as "eat, ate, full." On another, asked to use "knack" in a sentence, Mr. Kaplan had declaimed: "Bloom gives me a pain in the knack.")

8

Nostalgia wrapped Mr. Parkhill in its shroud. He started to open the back window when, quite without warning, the door flew open. A gust of air swept in from the corridor as a clarion voice proclaimed: "Hollo, averybody! Grittings!"

Twenty-six heads turned as one.

"Valcome to de new sizzon! Valcome to beginnis' grate!"

"Oy!" gasped Mrs. Moskowitz as of yore.

"I dun't believe it!" cried Mrs. Shimmelfarb.

"Lookit who's here!" rejoiced Mr. Pinsky.

"Holy smoky," frowned Mr. Isaac Nussbaum, who had but recently immigrated from the Holy Land.

Mr. Parkhill did not have to turn to identify the voice that had trumpeted "Grittings!" He could not mistake that enunciation, that supreme (if unwarranted) aplomb, that blithe, triumphant spirit. Besides, what other student would bid "Valcome!" to those who, enjoying prior residence, should clearly have welcomed him? Mr. Parkhill knew only one man who entered a classroom as if come for coronation.

"Mr."—his eyes found the ebullient entrant—"Kaplan. Well, well, Mr. Kaplan!"

It *was* Mr. Kaplan, proud, undaunted, a knight returned to the field of glory. He looked a whit more debonair, a mite more euphoric. He was sunburned, which so accented the natural luminosity of his skin that a light seemed to be shining under his apple-shaped cheeks. And he was freckled! How odd. Mr. Kaplan, the very epitome of urban civilization, freckled. For one absurd moment, Mr. Parkhill thought the freckles were shaped like stars, so that Mr. Kaplan's countenance advertised his name as he always wrote it—the letters in red, outlined in blue, the stars green: H*Y*M*A*N K*A*P*L*A*N. Mr. Parkhill repressed this foolish fantasy.

"Hollo, Mr. Pockheel! Harre you?" Mr. Kaplan was beaming. "Oh, I'm so heppy to see you I ken't tell abot!" Mr. Parkhill found himself shaking Mr. Kaplan's hand somewhat numbly. "You lookink fine! Foist-cless! A-Number-Vun!"

"You—er—look fine yourself." Mr. Parkhill cleared his throat. "Just splendid."

"I *fill* splandid."

"I—I'm glad to see you back, Mr. Kaplan."

"I'm besite you mit joy!"

Mr. Parkhill started to say "It's 'I'm beside *myself*,' Mr. Kaplan," but it was too late: Mr. Kaplan had turned to address his classmates: "Fallow students in beginnis' grate, ve vill voik togadder! Ve vill slafe! Ve vill *loin!*" He raised an imperial finger to the heavens. "Vun for all an' all for vun an' de whole kitten cadoodle for Mr. Pockheel!"

"Welcome home, Napoleon," said Mr. Blattberg bitterly, touching his amulet, the watch chain from which his heirs' baby teeth glittered.

Mr. Kaplan's gaze swept across subversive Blattberg, whom he did not deign to answer. "Ah, Mitnick! An' Nat'-an P. Nat'an! Bote still in beginnis' grate?! A plazent soprise. . . ."

The fawn, flushed out of her thicket, stammered, "H-hello, Mr. Kaplan."

Mr. Nathan laughed.

"I soggest for dis toim, Mitnick—"

"Do take a seat," said Mr. Parkhill hastily.

Mr. Kaplan strode to the chair in the center of the front row. "Pinsky."

Mr. Pinsky chortled, "Keplen!"

"I believe you occupy mine sitt." Mr. Kaplan said it without the slightest tinge of displeasure, but in the manner of a lord of the realm, asserting eminent domain.

At once, Mr. Pinsky gathered up his textbook, his notebook, his pencils, and slid into the seat beyond. He appeared honored to surrender the hallowed place, a shield-bearer who had been holding the castle keep against upstarts.

"Thot mon," moaned Miss Tarnova, shooting a poisonous glance at her enemy, "is a davil!"

"Now, class . . ." Mr. Parkhill quickly called.

The students at the board had so been beguiled by the fanfare that attended Hyman Kaplan's entrance that they had abandoned their autobiographies. They were giving the prodigal son ripe smiles, if friend, or frigid salutations, if foe. Those who were neither friend nor foe, like the Messrs. Wodjik, seemed paralyzed.

"Let us get back to our work," said Mr. Parkhill. "Mr. Kaplan will be with us for quite a while."

"Alvays," murmured Mr. Kaplan.

The image of Mr. Kaplan in the front row forever, unchanged, unchangeable, caused Mr. Parkhill to wince.

As the seven at the board returned to their labors, Mr. Kaplan took one of his fountain pens out of his outer breast pocket, narrowed his eyes, scanned the titles on the board with lightning dispatch, cocked his head to one side, whispered "Aha! So is de homevoik abot pest livink!" and began scribbling on an envelope furiously. Mr. Parkhill wondered what on earth he had seen to make him start scribbling away so *soon.*

"Let us finish, Blackboard . . ." (Mr. Parkhill wondered why in the world he, like other teachers, fell into the habit of characterizing students by their location. "Blackboard . . ." that was silly. He did not call the rest of the class "Chairs.")

The seven completed their transcription, returning to their seats with alibis and apologies. There was merit in their unconfidence.

Miss Lopez, ignoring the possessive adjective "my," had forsaken her life for a "Story of Life." Stanislaus Wilkomirski, bored by his past, had expatiated on "My Wife" instead of "My Life." Miss Tarnova, true to Mother Russia, had addressed herself to "Life. Death. *What They*

Mean???" Mr. Umea had composed a confessional which consisted of but three trenchant lines:

> Come N.Y. since 6 years.
> Work in lather belts.
> Marry. feel nice in morning.

Mr. Parkhill did not glance at the other compositions. He was quite disappointed. "Let us take Miss Lopez's work first. Corrections?"

At once Lola Lopez lowered her head; she looked like a sparrow. Her colleagues sat silent.

"Mistakes?" asked Mr. Parkhill lightly.

No critic stirred.

"We need not feel so—er—shy, class. We *learn* from our mistakes. . . . Anyone?"

No one.

Mr. Parkhill looked hopefully toward Miss Mitnick. Miss Mitnick blushed. He glanced toward Mr. Fledermann. C. J. Fledermann was sharpening his pencil. Mr. Parkhill smiled at Nathan P. Nathan, who winked back, but volunteered nothing.

Now, Mr. Parkhill gazed encouragingly at Rochelle Goldberg, but Miss Goldberg was unwrapping a caramel. Mr. Kaplan? Mr. Kaplan was still scribbling away on that precious envelope, which he had split open to double its area. What *had* gotten into the class tonight?

Bereft of participants, Mr. Parkhill corrected Miss Lopez's homework himself. And he proceeded to rectify the other autobiographies with speed. He seemed in a hurry.

Another batch of students was sent to the board. "Mrs. Pilpul. . . . Peter Studniczka . . ."

Suddenly Mr. Kaplan's splayed envelope wig-wagged in the air. "Mr. Pockheel! Mr. Pockheel!" The man's smile was as spacious as it was seductive. "Ken I go, plizz?"

Mr. Parkhill averted his gaze. "We are doing our *home*work, Mr. Kaplan. You were not here when I assigned—"

"I jost findished it! In dis exect spot!"

Mr. Pinsky exclaimed "Pssh!" and slapped both cheeks in awe.

Mr. Nathan laughed. "He will *kill* me!"

"You—uh—wrote your autobiography *here?*" asked Mr. Parkhill.

"De whole voiks!" Mr. Kaplan leaped from his seat to the board, seized a piece of chalk and, before Mr. Parkhill could protest or demur or dissuade, printed:

<u>Hyman Kaplan</u>
by
<u>H*Y*M*A*N K*A*P*L*A*N</u>

The title hypnotized Mr. Parkhill. How had Mr. Kaplan decided where to place the stars? In the first "Hyman Kaplan"? That would imply that it was the *idea* of Mr. Kaplan, not the real Mr. Kaplan, that was all-important. In both "Hyman Kaplan"s? That would suggest a split personality. But putting the stars only in the second "Hyman Kaplan," as Mr. Kaplan had done—that, Mr. Parkhill had to concede, was masterful: for it emphasized Kaplan the man, not Kaplan the subject; Kaplan the creator, not Kaplan the concept.

Mr. Parkhill forced his eyes away from Mr. Kaplan's composition to scan the work of his companions at the board. Mr. Blattberg was copying an epic entitled "Who I am!" Miss Kipnis was baring her soul in a saga called, somewhat mysteriously, "Riga 47." (It turned out that "Riga 47" referred to the city and zone of "Cookie" Kipnis's nativity.) Most surprising was the composition, if that was what it was, of Peter Ignatius Studniczka; he had poured the story of his life into a skeletonic mold:

Moth. & Fath.	Mary & Frank
broth.	6
sist.	<u>3</u>

broths & sists	9
dead	2 (sist.)
Wife	No
childs	not
job	bottel washr
want be	Bottel Boss

Mr. Parkhill turned his back to the board. He waited for them all to finish, and he heard them return to their seats, one by one. "Let us begin with"—he took a deep breath—"Mr. Kaplan." Only then did he summon the fortitude to confront the full flowering of Mr. Kaplan's soul:

<u>Hyman Kaplan</u>
by
H*Y*M*A*N K*A*P*L*A*N

First, I was born.
In Kiev, in old contry. (Moishe Elman, famous on fiddle, was also coming from Kiev.)

"Notice the sentence structure, class," said Mr. Parkhill absently. (His mind was not on sentence structure at all: it was wrestling with the impeccable logic of "First, I was born.")

My father had the name Joe but freinds were calling him Yussel. My mother had the name Ida, but I called her Mama. Netcheral.

"Watch for errors in spelling," intoned Mr. Parkhill.

Also was 4 brothers and sisters. Avrum, Mireleh, me (my name was Hymie), Becky. Behind Becky came Max. That Max! He is tarrible smart. He got a wonderful mamory, only he forgats.

"Pay attention to the *meaning* of the sentences," Mr. Parkhill called resolutely.

14

Came bad times (plenty) so I took 5 year to get my Visa and saled to wonderful U.S. Took 10 days, and sick also 10 days. I falt sure is allready "Goodbye, Hyman Kaplan!"

"And note the quotation marks!" Mr. Parkhill blurted in alarm.

In N.Y. I am heppy. But not 100%. So I am coming to school. To learn. All. I am full all kinds embition. My mottol is—"Kaplan, GO HIGH!!"

T-h-e E-n-d

"The end . . ." Mr. Parkhill studied the floor; he knew it was only the beginning.

Hummings and buzzings and *sotto voce* gloats passed across the scholars' ranks, as they did whenever Mr. Kaplan displayed his prose.

Mr. Parkhill tapped his pointer on the desk. "Now, class. . . . Corrections."

They leaped to the onslaught with gusto. Mr. Blattberg denounced Mr. Kaplan for mutilating four entirely innocent words: " 'freinds . . . contry . . . mamory . . . embition.' " Miss Atrakian deplored the lawlessness of Mr. Kaplan's verbs, which wandered from the present to the participial without a shred of respect for the past. Mr. Fledermann exclaimed: "This man makes *backwarts* hiss quotation points! Front ones are back ones, and back ones are dizzy!" (A chorus fit for Berlioz praised C. J. Fledermann for this subtle observation.)

Miss Ziev remodeled one sentence with scorn and removed two periods with contempt. Even Molly Yanoff, smoothing her eternal black frock, caught Mr. Kaplan in flagrant error: "Who *don't* call a Mama 'Mama'? So is that 'but' after 'Ida' foolish, I think, no?" Mr. Hruska (who had entered without fanfare) grunted that "mottol" should be "motel." As for Reuben Olansky, this new Hector smote Achilles in both heels, firing scathing salvos at the malapropisms Hyman Kaplan had spawned and voicing condo-

15

lences to the diction he had massacred.

"Hyman Kaplan by H*Y*M*A*N K*A*P*L*A*N" bled.

As Mr. Parkhill's chalk raced across the board—correcting, deleting, transposing, replacing—he could not help observing that the entire class, so subdued but half an hour ago, was bursting with vitality. Whatever you might say about Mr. Kaplan, his presence could resuscitate a corpse.

"Any more mistakes?" Mr. Parkhill asked buoyantly.

Miss Mitnick stammered, "In the composition I think are mistakes also in *meaning!*"

"Good," grinned Mr. Nathan.

"Prosidd, Mitnick," Mr. Kaplan murmured, turning inscrutable.

"Should not be a musician in this homework!" Demure Miss Mitnick, who had suffered so many wounds in confrontations with Hyman Kaplan, was careful to address this statement to Mr. Parkhill: "Why does Mr. Kaplan put Mischa Elman in the story of his own life?"

"I like his playink," smiled Mr. Kaplan.

"Hanh?!" wheezed Mr. Olansky. "That's a *reason—?!*"

"No. It's a decision!"

"Oh boy!" Mr. Pinsky slapped his thigh in elation.

Miss Mitnick had begun to whinny, which so alarmed Stanislaus Wilkomirski that the gallant Pole dashed to befriend her. "No, not right!" he protested. "Is *not* got a place in your life—like lady say!"

"I vant Moishe Elman in mine life," said Mr. Kaplan. "In *your* life put Paderewski."

Mr. Wilkomirski fled the field.

"Stop!" cried C. J. Fledermann, riding in Wilkomirski's stead. "I happen to be a music teacher!"

The appearance of Gabriel could have generated no greater acclamation. "A *teacher!*"

"In our class!!"

16

Isaac Nussbaum surmised: "He must be high educated," and stroked his beard in homage.

"Elman's name was 'Mischa,' not 'Moishe'!" snapped Christian Fledermann.

"It dipands on who's prononcink," said Mr. Kaplan.

"*Mr.* Kap—"

Suddenly, Miss Tarnova cried, "From *my* homeland came Tchaikovsky, Borodin—"

"Also Resputin," crooned her nemesis.

"Rachmaninoff! Moussorgsky!"

"Crazy Kink Piter."

"Stravin—"

"Miss Tarnova—" Mr. Parkhill cut in, realizing that Miss Tarnova could go on all night cataloguing Russia's immortals, and Mr. Kaplan his roster of maniacs. "Suppose we get on with our *correc*tions."

Up shot the hand of Reuben Olansky. "I see an *important* piece of mish-mosh!"

Mr. Kaplan wheeled around to face this new peasant.

"What kind of *sanse,*" Mr. Olansky inquired acidly, "is in a student who can write—right there"—he thrust an accusatory forefinger at the board (unfortunately he was lunging at Miss Kipnis's memoir, so askew was his vision) —"that 'Max had a wonderful memory, only he forgets'?! Isn't that ridiculouse?"

The Philistines rocked in merriment.

"That's like saying a man is fat but skinny!" boomed stern Olansky. "A millionaire but poor!"

The chamber shook with hilarity.

"Good for Olansky!"

"Brilliant rizzoning!"

"Ooo Kaplan!" jeered Mrs. Moskowitz, disciplining her diphthong.

"Vouldn't you say—'poor Kaminsky'?" purred Mr. Kaplan.

17

"Who?"

"Why Kaminsky?!"

"Class! . . . Mr. Kaplan . . ." Mr. Parkhill's palms were perspiring. "Mr. Olansky is quite right. I fail to see your point about—er—"

"Kaminsky."

"—Mr. Kaminsky."

Mr. Kaplan shrugged. "Harry Kaminsky is a furrier on mine block. He has t'ree odder stores. The man is a malted millionaire, an' still—"

"Multi-million—"

"—he's in hospital, mit hiccups! Sofferink tarrible! So vouldn't even Olansky say 'Poor Kaminsky'?"

A storm rattled the walls.

"A treek!"

"Kaminsky is *rich,* not poor!" shouted Mr. Hruska.

"Rich and sick, not *poor* and sick!" blushed Miss Mitnick.

"That guy is a whiz-bank!" chortled Mr. Nathan.

"Class, *class!*" Mr. Parkhill's pointer was pounding an admonitory tattoo. "Mr. Kaplan, your example does *not* refute Mr. Olansky. 'Poor millionaire,' as you used it, is just a—colloquial way of putting it. You call him 'poor' to show sympathy, not to describe his—er—wealth. Let us stick to Mr. Olansky's criticism of your statement about your brother: that is, that he has a wonderful memory, but forgets. That, Mr. Kaplan, is a flat contradiction!"

"Ahh," leered Hyman Kaplan.

"What's with this 'Aah?'" demanded Reuben Olansky. (He could hardly be blamed for not knowing that Mr. Kaplan considered a contradiction an achievement, not an error.)

"Mr. Kaplan," frowned Mr. Parkhill, "that statement is not—logical!"

"Not *logical?*" Mr. Kaplan reeled. For Mr. Kaplan to be

18

accused of illogic was tantamount to Titian's being charged with color-blindness.

"Give an inch, Mr. Kaplan, give an *inch,*" pleaded Bessie Shimmelfarb.

Instead of yielding an inch, Mr. Kaplan raised a ruler. "Vhy is it not logical?"

Miss Mitnick exclaimed, "How can your brother have a wonderful memory if—as you say—he *forgets?*"

Mr. Kaplan eyed her with infinite pity. "My brodder Mex heppens to possass a movvelous mamory—"

"But you yourself admit he forgets."

"Occasionally."

"But if he f-forgets—"

"Mex is only human."

"—either he has a *good* memory, and remembers, or a *bad* memory, and forgets!" Miss Mitnick's state was heart-rending.

"Correct!" called Nathan P. Nathan.

"Koplon is tropped," intoned Olga Tarnova.

"Give Mr. Keplen a chence!" sputtered faithful Pinsky.

Mr. Kaplan crossed the Rubicon. "Mine dear Mitnick," he murmured, "I regrat your pars of rizzoning. . . . *Is* a mamory eider good or bed? Is a day eider boilink or friz-zink?" His glance impaled Reuben Olansky. "Is Life so tsimple? Is Man so cotton dry?"

" 'Cut-and-*dried.' "

"Batter *t'ink* abot dis, Olansky! T'ink *dipper,* Mitnick!" Mr. Kaplan illustrated how to "t'ink dipper" by narrowing only one eye whilst cauterizing his inquisitors with the other. "Fects are fects! Foist, my brodder has a vunderful mamory! Like a policeman! But—*sometimes* Mex forgats. So does dat minn he doesn't have a movvelous mamory *ven ve jost agreet he did?!*"

It was outrageous. It was grotesque. It made sophistry ashamed of itself. And it plunged the classroom into pandemonium. Mr. Olansky bellowed protestations. Mrs. Pilpul was seized by vertigo. Mrs. Moskowitz complained of hot flushes. Miss Mitnick verged on tears. (Poor Miss Mitnick: once more right, yet once more routed.)

"God alsmighty!" roared two Wodjiks as one.

"Denk you," said Mr. Kaplan.

"Class—"

"*Cu*ckoo! *Cu*ckoo!" Miss Goldberg dived for a chocolate cream.

Christian J. Fledermann was so speechless that he put his head in his hands and brayed.

"Kapalan belongs in the *movies!*" caroled Nathan P. Nathan.

"He belongs in prison!" raged Mr. Blattberg.

Mr. Parkhill's rapping pointer and loudest voice quelled the broil and babble. "Ladies! Gentlemen! Attention, everyone!" The tumult subsided. "We must not let ourselves be—carried away. Criticism does not require quarreling. Let me return to the point at issue." He looked squarely at the man who had (once more) set off an explosion. "Mr. Kaplan"—Mr. Parkhill made no effort to exclude asperity from his tone—"you have simply twisted the facts! You have evaded the excellent objections raised by Mr. Olansky and Miss Mitnick. They are absolutely right. *You* are absolutely—in error!"

Mr. Kaplan looked crestfallen. The Mitnick-Olansky-Tarnova platoon preened in satisfaction.

"Let me retrace the argument step by step." Mr. Parkhill conducted his autopsy with merciless strokes. He *could* not permit Mr. Kaplan to employ such chicanery. He would not let reason be smothered by casuistry. He had seen his bravest, brightest scholars fall before Mr. Kaplan's blunderbuss. . . . Mr. Parkhill split Mr. Kaplan's offending sentence into two clearly opposed parts. He slashed the *non sequitur* to ribbons. He exposed the assertion *a priori* and deposed it *a posteriori*. *This* time, only the second night out on the new term's voyage, Mr. Parkhill was determined that Mr. Kaplan not be allowed to wiggle out of error by outrageous sophistry.

And an odd thing happened. Even as he chastised his most intractable pupil, Mr. Parkhill felt nourishing juices course through his veins. For the priceless spark of life, the very heart of learning, had been revived in what, but half an hour ago, had been a dull and listless congregation.

As he revealed each cunning nuance of the pettifoggery with which Mr. Kaplan had confounded his adversaries, Mr. Parkhill caught himself feeling grateful that Hyman Kaplan—nay, H·Y·M·A·N K·A·P·L·A·N—had come home again.

2

CHRISTOPHER C. K·A·P·L·A·N

To Mr. Parkhill the beginners' grade was more than a group of adults yearning to learn English. He took a larger view of his responsibilities: to Mr. Parkhill the school was an incubator of Citizens. To imbue men and women from a dozen nations with the meaning of America—its dramatic past, its precious traditions, its noblest aspirations—this, to Mr. Parkhill, was the greater work to which he had dedicated himself.

So it was that on the eve of any national holiday, Mr. Parkhill opened the class session with a little excursion into American history. In the spring, it was Decoration Day that enlisted his eloquence. In the fall, it was Thanksgiving. (He always regretted the fact that the Fourth of July, grandest holiday of them all, fell in a month when the school was not open.) And this Monday night in October, on the eve of Columbus Day, Mr. Parkhill began with these ringing words: "Tonight, class, let us set aside our routine tasks for a while to discuss the man whose historic achievement our country will commemorate tomorrow."

Expectancy welled up in the air.

"To this man," said Mr. Parkhill, "America owes its very beginning. I'm sure you all know whom I mean—"

"Jawdgie Washington!" Isaac Nussbaum promptly guessed.

"No, not 'Georgie'—*George*—Washington. I was referring to another—"

"Cortez?" asked Lola Lopez. "Ricardo Cortez?"

"That's a moom-picture actor!" Nathan P. Nathan could hardly contain his laughter.

"N-no, Miss Lopez. It was *Hernando* Cortez who—er—came somewhat later than the historic figure to whom I—"

"Paul Rewere!" cried Oscar Trabish.

Mr. Parkhill adjusted his glasses. Mr. Trabish had formed a peculiar psychic union with "Paul Rewere": he had already written two rhapsodic compositions and made one speech of tribute to his beloved alter ego. (The written eulogies had been named "Paul Revere's Horse Makes History" and "Paul Revere: One by Land, Two by Beach." The speech had been announced by Mr. Trabish as "Paul Rewere! Why He Wasn't Prazidant?" He had been quite indignant about it.)

"Not Paul 'Rewere,' " sighed Mr. Parkhill. "It's a 'v,' Mr. Trabish, not a 'w.' You *spell* it correctly, but you replace the 'v's with 'w's—and the 'w's with 'v's—when you speak. . . . Class, let's not just guess. What *date* is tomorrow?"

"Mine boitday!" an excited tenor sang out.

Mr. Parkhill ignored that. "I'll give you a hint." He smiled hintfully. "Tomorrow is October twelfth. And on October twelfth, in the year 1492—"

"Dat's mine *boit*day! October tvalf! I should live so! Mr. Pockheel, honest to Gott!"

It was (but why, oh why, did it have to be?) Hyman Kaplan.

Mr. Parkhill took a deep breath. "Mr. Kaplan," he asked warily, "is October twelfth—*really* your birthday?"

"*Mis*ter Pockheel!"

Mr. Parkhill felt ashamed of himself.

"Keplan is too old to have bird-days!" scowled Mr. Nussbaum, stroking his beard.

"October tvalf I'm born; October tvalf I'm tsalebratink!" retorted Mr. Kaplan. "All mine *life* I'm hevink boitdays on October tvalf. No axceptions!"

Mr. Parkhill said, "Well, well. That *is* a coincidence." He cleared his throat. "I'm sure we all wish Mr. Kaplan many happy returns."

"Heppy retoins!"

"Good lock!"

"You should live to a hondret!"

Messrs. Olansky and Fledermann sat silent, questioning whether Mr. Kaplan's longevity was an unalloyed blessing.

Mr. Kaplan acknowledged the felicitations: a beam, a little bow, a trio of "Denk you"s.

By this time, Miss Mitnick had conquered her shyness enough to call "Congratulation."

"That goes for me!" laughed Mr. Nathan.

"Mitnick." Mr. Kaplan inclined his head. "Nat'an."

"However," Mr. Parkhill raised his voice, "the particular *historical* event we shall commemorate tomorrow pertains to—Christopher Columbus. For it was on October twelfth, 1492—"

"*Colom*biss?" Mr. Kaplan's rapture burst its seams. "Christ*over Colom*biss?!"

Excitement seized the beginners' grade.

"Columbus!"

"Columbia Day," breathed Olga Tarnova. "Ah, Colombos. . . . Romohnteek."

"Colombus discovert America!" cried Mr. Pinsky, as if he had just discovered Columbus.

"Oy!" No one could groan a "What?" or moan a "Why?" with one-tenth the significance Sadie Moskowitz put into her "Oy"s. She was the Niobe of the beginners' grade.

"Yes, class, on October twelfth, 1492—"

Mr. Trabish dropped a sneer in the general direction of

24

Isaac Nussbaum. "And you said George Washington! Heh!"

"*You* sad Paul Rewere! Phooey!"

"Phooey!" echoed Mr. Hruska.

"On October twelfth, 1492—" Mr. Parkhill tried again.

"By me could every day in the year be something about Paul Rewere!" proclaimed Oscar Trabish.

"And by *me* is our first Prezident worth ten men on a horse!" retorted Isaac Nussbaum.

Lucca Barbella cried, *"Bravo!"*

Miss Goldberg reached for a sourball.

"On October twelfth, 1492"—Mr. Parkhill's tone brooked no ignoring—"Christopher Columbus discovered a new continent! Setting sail in three small ships—"

A hush gripped the grade as Mr. Parkhill launched into the deathless saga of Christopher Columbus and the brave little armada that challenged the unknown. He spoke slowly, impressively. (It was not often he was afforded material of such majesty.) And his novitiates, caught in the drama of that great and fearful voyage, hung upon every syllable. "The food ran low. Water was scarce. Rumors of doom—of disaster, of fatal reefs or fearful sea monsters—raced through the frightened crew. . . ."

Shirley Ziev leaned forward to sigh into Mr. Kaplan's ear: "You are lucky, Mr. Kaplan. Born the same day Columbus did."

Mr. Kaplan was in the world of dreams. He kept whispering "Christover Colombiss" to himself, transported. "My!" He closed his eyes. "October tvalf I'm arrivink in de voild, an' October tvalf Colombiss picks ot for discoverink a new world. . . . Dastiny!"

"Mutiny faced Christopher Columbus," Mr. Parkhill intoned with feeling. "His officers begged him—"

"My boithday is Motch toity," sighed Miss "Cookie" Kip-

nis in envy. "Not even a soborb was discovered Motch toity!"

Mr. Kaplan comforted desolate Kipnis. "Ufcawss, Colombiss discovert a *long* time bifore Keplen iven breeded."

"October twalf is October twalf!" cried ever-loyal Pinsky.

Mr. Kaplan allowed the mantle of history to fall upon his shoulders.

Mr. Parkhill, upon whom the Ziev-Kipnis-Pinsky symposium had not been lost, described the geographical illusions of Europeans in 1492, the belief that the world was flat as a plate, the mockery to which proud Columbus had been subjected. He traced the ironic confluence of events through which two continents had been named after Amerigo Vespucci.

"Dey are called Naut an' Sot America by *mistake?*" exclaimed Mr. Kaplan, doubting his ears, and at once answered his own question with an indignant, "By mistake!" It was clear he would never forgive Vespucci.

Mr. Parkhill proceeded with determination, recounting the crisis of that immortal voyage, three tiny ships on an ocean infested, in men's minds, by demons of the deep. He extolled the fortitude of the captain who would not turn back. He described the awful night when Columbus prayed for God's guidance once more, and decided that unless land was seen the next morn he would turn back. . . . And when Mr. Parkhill whispered, "And then a voice from the crow's-nest cried 'Land! Land!' " gasps of relief vied with gulps of gratitude in the transfixed grade. A tear rolled down Miss Mitnick's cheek. When Mr. Parkhill described the landing on Bahamian soil, Miss Tarnova inhaled the scent of her kerchief and Miss Atrakian suppressed a sob. And when their earnest shepherd said, "And because Columbus thought he was really in India, he called the natives Indians . . ." the amazement of his flock surpassed description.

"Vun mistake on top de odder!" cried Kaplan.

"Dey called *Hindyans* by mistake?" gasped Mrs. Moskowitz. Mrs. Moskowitz could not believe that of history.

"Yes, Mrs. Moskowitz, Indians—by mistake."

Mr. Kaplan shook his head. "Dose poor Indians."

Miss Lopez fingered her beads.

Mr. Parkhill hurried on to the role of Ferdinand and Isabella. Just as he was about to complete *that* absorbing tale, Mr. Kaplan announced, "Ectual, ve ain't iven Amaricans!"

Mr. Parkhill paused. " 'Actual*ly,* we *are*n't *e*ven Americans,' Mr. Kaplan. There is no such word as 'ain't.' "

"Actual*ly,* we all Colombians!" A demand for justice—long overdue—burned in Hyman Kaplan's eyes.

"Now you're talking!" called stout Pinsky.

Mr. Parkhill turned the class over to Miss Mitnick for General Discussion. This was an innovation on Mr. Parkhill's part. General Discussion was very popular with his students, and a fruitful exercise to boot; and it was particularly productive when he delegated one of the more competent pupils to lead it. None excelled Rose Mitnick in ability. Whether she was as pleased as she was nervous, as she stumbled up the aisle, no one could say; that she was as pale as a turnip, no one could deny.

Mr. Parkhill took a seat in the back of the room, as he always did during General Discussion (or Recitation and Speech). Miss Mitnick mounted the platform on which Mr. Parkhill's desk stood, her cheeks incarnadined, passing a trembling hand across her trembling hair. She lowered herself in Authority's chair. Mr. Nathan laughed encouragement; Mrs. Yanoff applauded; the widow Pilpul called, "Don't be ascared!"

That, of course, trebled Miss Mitnick's trepidation. Eyes glazed, she stammered: "F-fellow s-students . . ."

"Spik netcherel," whispered Hyman Kaplan.

"Thank you—"

"You velcome."

"—it is an honor and also a p-privilege to open, by Mr. Parkhill's own choosing, General D-discussion!"

"Oh, Rose Mitnick!" moist-eyed Moskowitz breathed.

"Mr. Parkhill has told us the wonderful story of Columbus. So maybe we—his students in beginners' grade—should begin with paying s-special attention to . . . ." Miss Mitnick struck the keynote for the rest of the evening with a touching tribute to explorers in general and Columbus in particular. She ended her tribute with what Mr. Parkhill thought was a most deft comparison of Columbus and Admiral Byrd. "Both men found new worlds for humanity!"

"Edmiral *Boyd?*" Mr. Kaplan promptly echoed in disdain. "Who is dis all-of-a-sodden hero?"

"He discovered the South Pole!" exclaimed Miss Mitnick.

"*Him* you compare mit Col*om*biss?!" Astonishment joined umbrage in Mr. Kaplan's tone. "An Edmiral *Boyd?!*"

"It's '*Ad*miral *Byrd*,' " Mr. Parkhill called.

"He was a kind of modern Columbus," Miss Mitnick blurted. "*He* also went to a new continent—"

"Vhat kind continent? Only snow, ice an' funny pigeons!"

" '*Pen*guins!' "

"But he was the *first* one," Miss Mitnick started, "who—"

"Somvun vas foist to make popcorn, so do ve have a holiday in his honor?!"

"I'll *die!*" choked Nathan P. Nathan.

"Mr. Kap—"

"Admiral Byrd was a *hero!*" cried Rose Mitnick. "He did discover the whole South Pole!"

"Som discoverink!" sniffed Mr. Kaplan, dismissing all of Antarctica.

"Stop!" boomed Reuben Olansky, his lenses magnifying

his ferocity. "South Pole is very important!"

"Ha! Averyvun *knew* dere vas a Pole in de sot!" Mr. Kaplan said. "All Edmiral Boyd did vas go dere!"

Miss Mitnick turned amber, Mr. Fledermann turned blue, and Bessie Shimmelfarb pleaded, "Give an *inch,* Mr. Kaplan, give an *inch.*"

"Kaplan, are you *crazy?*" Mr. Blattberg flung a sentiment concurred in by many.

"He is not normal," opined Mr. Nussbaum.

"An' Edmiral Boyd *vas?* To go t'ousants of miles to a place vhere all you can do is prectice frizzink?"

"Class—"

Mr. Olansky was so furious that he turned his back upon Mr. Kaplan and addressed scathing protestations to the side wall: "Minerals. . . . Panguins. . . . An achievement for *Science.* . . . Koplan turns it all hopside down!!"

"I," murmured Mr. Kaplan, "don't say 'hopside' for 'opside.' "

Mr. Nathan howled.

"Gentlemen . . ." Mr. Parkhill chided them. "Please. . . . Proceed, Miss Mitnick."

Miss Mitnick, who had been biting her lip and fluttering her hands, reshouldered her duties. "In *spite* Mr. Kaplan's remark that everybody *knew* was a South Pole and Admiral Byrd only went there, we all agree he was a big hero. He soffered terrible things for humanity: cold, icebergs, alone below zero—"

"Edmiral Boyd vent mit all modinn conveniences!" cried Mr. Kaplan.

"Yos!" blurted Tomas Wodjik, to everyone's surprise.

"He even spent money for hitting goils!" affirmed Milas Wodjik.

The by-now tautened nerves of the scholars snapped into smithereens.

"Lie!"

29

"Shame!"

"Take back those woids!"

It took the hasty intervention of Mr. Parkhill, from the back row, to clarify the confusion (in which he, too, floundered). Tomas Wodjik explained that when his twin, Milas, an expert electrician but maladroit speaker, had said "hitting goils" he meant Admiral Byrd had been supplied with "heating coils."

"Oh migott!" croaked Mr. Nussbaum.

"Heating coils?!" Nathan P. Nathan slapped Mr. Pinsky's back in jubilation.

"Some cless," sighed Mr. Kaplan.

"Gentlemen! Class. . . . Thank you, Mr. Wodjik. I'm glad you explained that." Mr. Parkhill was more than glad; he was overjoyed. The thought that Admiral Byrd had spent government funds to smuggle girls to the South Pole so that he could flagellate them at his leisure was too dreadful to contemplate. "Miss Mitnick, please resume the discussion."

As Miss Mitnick made noises of strangulation, Lucca Barbella erupted: "Is only da one Cristoforo Colombo! Is only da one Amerigo Vespucci! Is noa one lak—befora, behinda!" To Mr. Barbella, beyond any peradventure of doubt, Columbus and Vespucci, wholly Italian titans, would never be matched, much less outshone. Admiral Byrd, he said flatly, was merely a "copying cat."

"Right!" beamed Mr. Kaplan.

"Class . . ."

Miss Mitnick tapped Mr. Parkhill's desk tearfully. "Order. . . . The discussion must go farther. . . . Who would like to ask the floor?"

Olaf Umea demanded the floor, and took it before Miss Mitnick could give it to him. "Columbus was a great man! No doubts about!" Columbus was indeed worth all that Mr. Kaplan and Miss Mitnick had claimed for him. But, Mr.

Umea glowered, how could any student of history consider Columbus more than a vapid descendant of the greatest explorer of them all: Leif Ericson? (The Viking, it turned out, was born no more than a handful of kilometers from the birthplace of Olaf Umea.)

"Boit *days* are more important den *boitplaces!*" Mr. Kaplan promptly proclaimed.

The advocate from Scandinavia blustered and muttered, "And don't even *mention* that Vestpucci, a liar—"

"No, no!" shouted Mr. Barbella. "Amerigo Vespucci was born in Italia also!"

"So was Marcus Polo," retorted Mr. Kaplan, "an' he got lost in Chinaton!"

"Class—"

"*Diavolo! Assassino! Bugiardo!*"

"Are ve salabratink Colombiss Day or making spaghetti?" asked Mr. Kaplan.

"Anyone else wants the floor?" entreated Miss Mitnick. "Mr.—Nathan?!"

Nathan P. Nathan was wiping tears from his eyes. "No, thanks, Rose."

"Miss Goldberg?" pleaded Miss Mitnick.

"Zln mb thnks," came through Miss Goldberg's taffy-coated mouth.

"Mr.—"

"—Keplen," completed the name's owner helpfully.

"*Any*one! The floor is absolutely *open,*" Miss Mitnick announced, but denied her offer by keeping her eyes where Mr. Kaplan's could not possibly meet them. "*Any*body can talk."

No one but her arch-enemy seemed willing to talk.

"Mr. Wodjik?!" asked plaintive Miss Mitnick.

Milas Wodjik hemmed as Tomas Wodjik hawed.

"Mrs. Pilpul?"

The widow gulped in the negative.

31

"Lest call for volunteers!" panted Miss Mitnick.

Up rose the sole volunteer. "Foidinand an' Isabel. Ha!" Mr. Kaplan sat down.

Uneasy murmurings swept through the tiers.

Miss Mitnick stammered, "I didn't c-catch."

Mr. Kaplan made gracious allowance for Miss Mitnick's impediment. "I sad, 'Foidinand an' Isabel—Ha!'"

"Why he makes ha-ha on royalties?!" cried "Cookie" Kipnis.

"Thot mon is mod . . . mod," moaned Miss Tarnova.

"Mr. Kap—"

"Exaplain to Miss Mitnick!" Mr. Nathan demanded, grinning.

"Describe your exact meaning dose remocks!" the voice of Aaron Blattberg rang out. (Such clarity and persistence had made Aaron Blattberg a crackerjack shirt salesman on Avenue B.)

Mr. Kaplan smiled, silent and inscrutable.

"Koplan wants to explain, or Koplan wants to take back?" fumed Mr. Olansky, addressing the ceiling.

"Y-yes, Mr. Kaplan," called Mr. Parkhill. "I do think the class is entitled to *some* explanation—"

"All of a sodden he makes fun Foidinand Isabel!" protested Mrs. Moskowitz. "Not even saying 'Axcuse'? Is this a way to tritt kinks and quinns?!"

The frontal attack stirred the royalists into action.

"Talk, Kaplan!"

"You got the floor."

"Tell awreddy!"

"Mr. Kaplan . . ." Miss Mitnick quavered.

In response to the public demand he had cunningly created, Mr. Kaplan rose once more. "Ladies, gantleman, Mr. Pockheel, chairlady . . ." Miss Mitnick lowered her lashes. "Ve all agree dat Colombiss's joiney vas vun of de most movvelous t'ings aver happened in de voild." Nods,

32

clucks, grunts (however reluctant). *"T'ink* abot dat treep . . . jost *t'ink*. Viks an' viks Colombiss vas sailink—sailink t'rough tarrible storms, lighteninks, tonder. T'rough vafes as high as de Umpire State Buildink. Fodder an' fodder Colombiss vent—not afraid, not belivink in monasters of de dip, crossink dat onchotted ocean, not yildink to t'rets of ravolution fromm his screws." The new Herodotus paused to let the awesome data sink home. "Vell, my frands, in *vat kind boats* did Colombiss made dat vunderful voyitch?" His eyes became slits. "In strong, fency boats? In plazant accommodations? No! In leetle, teentsy vassals. Chizz-boxes! Sheeps full of likks! Boats full of doit, joims, vater commink in! *Som* boats for discoverink Amarica!" Mr. Kaplan's indignation curdled the air. "An' dats vhy I'm sayink, *'Shame* on you, Foidinand! *Shame* on you, Isabel!' " The bright blue eyes flashed. "Couldn't dey give a man like Colombiss batter transportation?"

"Shame!" cried sympathetic Pinsky.

"Olé, Columbus!" cried Miss Lopez, upon whom had just dawned the debt Iberia owed Columbus.

"Foolish talk," muttered Olaf Umea, visualizing the rude craft of Leif Ericson.

Now the opposition buckled on its armor.

"Lat the past alone!"

"Isabel *liked* Columbus!"

"Maybe in 1492 Koplan could manufacture a S.S. *Quinn Elizabat?*" Mr. Olansky asked the side wall acidly.

A storm of retorts, taunts, defenses and disclaimers rolled across the contentious ranks. Mr. Pinsky shouted that Mr. Kaplan was absolutely right; C. J. Fledermann snarled that Mr. Kaplan was demented. Miss Atrakian reminded Mr. Kaplan that Queen Isabella was not an interior decorator for a navy. Mrs. Moskowitz announced that she was having palpitations. Mr. Nathan tried to encourage Miss Mitnick with energetic winkings, but the wan moderator, staggering under the burdens of arbitration, wailed, "Mr. Kaplan, *please*. The ships Ferdinand and Isabella gave Mr. Columbus were f-fine for that *time*."

"For de *time?*" thundered Hyman Kaplan. "But not for de *man!*"

"But in those days—"

"A ginius like Colombiss should have averyting fromm de bast!"

"Oh, *gott!*" croaked Mr. Blattberg.

"Kaplen, give an *inch!*" pleaded Bessie Shimmelfarb.

"Right is right!" rejoined the sage. "I don't mashure de troot on a ruler!"

Miss Tarnova moaned, "Mr. Koplon is no gantlemon."

"He's a born lawyer!" blared Nathan P. Nathan.

Mr. Parkhill rose hastily. "Class, I think—"

"Colombiss desoived batter den a *Senta Maria,* a *Nina* an' a *Pintele!*" Mr. Kaplan declaimed, hacking left and right in behalf of his birth-mate. "Ven a man stotts ot to discover Amarica—"

"But Columbus didn't go out to discover a specific *place!*" Miss Mitnick protested.

"No?" Mr. Kaplan's mien dripped pity even as his ɔngue dripped honey. "Vhat did he go for? *Axercise?!*"

"I mean"—poor Miss Mitnick thrashed about in throes of desperation—"I mean that Columbus didn't *know* there was a continent in the middle Atlantic Ocean! Columbus just went out—"

Mr. Kaplan tendered her a forbearance laced with contempt. "Colombiss just 'vent ot'? . . . Vhy, dear Mitnick? Vhy did he vent ot?"

"To—to discover!"

"Vhat to discover?"

Miss Mitnick bleated, "Just—to *discover.*"

Mr. Kaplan surveyed the heated ranks, tolerant, nodding, the picture of patience contending with naïveté. "Colombiss just vent; he just vent to discover," he repeated. *"Just* to discover!" He glanced toward heaven, lamenting the limitations of human perspicacity. Then, face dark, he struck. "Som pipple t'ink dat if a man goes ot to mail a letter, he only *hopes* dat *maybe* he'll find a mailbox!"

"Stop!" howled Mr. Olansky, smiting his forehead.

"Oooy!" protested Sadie Moskowitz.

"Is-there-no-law-against-such-a-travesty-of-reasoning?' was all but inscribed on Mr. Umea's flabbergasted features.

And now the battle soared—with shouts and cries and accusations; with righteous assaults on the Kaplan logic, and impassioned defenses of the Mitnick virtue. Mr. Fledermann sputtered that Mr. Kaplan had pulled an unfair rabbit out of an illegal hat; Mr. Pinsky rejoined that C. J. Fledermann was too superficial to comprehend the profundity of Mr. Kaplan's ratiocinations. Mrs. Yanoff charged that Mr. Pinsky was nothing but a "Kaplan coolie"; Mr. Barbella averred that Mrs. Yanoff was but a myrmidon of Mitnick. Mr. Blattberg warned everyone that Mr. Kaplan would drive him crazy; "Cookie" Kipnis alleged that Mr. Blattberg's mental condition predated exposure to a man of Mr. Kaplan's stature. In a spate of scuffles on the sidelines, Mr. Wilkomirski blubbered, Mrs. Shimmelfarb pleaded, Miss Atrakian ranted, Mr. Trabish woke up, and the brothers Wodjik—shipwrecked—wandered in fraternal disorientation. As for Nathan P. Nathan, he was in convulsions. (Mr. Nathan seemed allergic to partisanship, so corruptible was he by entertainment.)

"Class!" Miss Mitnick implored them. "Please, every person!"

Mr. Parkhill was hurrying to his post in alarm.

Miss Goldberg, trying to dislodge a sourball she had misswallowed during the melee, began to both gag and gasp, "Slep my beck! Slep my beck!"

Mrs. Pilpul slapped her back just as the bell trilled in the corridor.

The bell went "Thrring!" and "Prring!" and "Thrrang!" but so ensnarled was the multitude in conflict that no one hearkened.

High above the furor, Mr. Parkhill called, "Dismissed! Class! That will be all!" He proclaimed it with total authority but inner misgivings.

For Mr. Parkhill could not help feeling that General Discussion had not been at all successful this evening. Yet how could he have known? . . . If only Columbus had discovered America on October eleventh! . . . If only Hyman Kaplan had been born on October thirteenth. . . .

3

THE DREADFUL DREAM
OF MR. PARKHILL

It was a splendid evening. The moon washed the city with silver, flowing down the proud spires into the pockmarked streets.

Mr. Parkhill consulted his watch. Forty minutes before he was due to meet his class. He had indulged in a rather heavy dinner (he did love Brown Betty); it would do him good to walk. He tucked his briefcase under his arm and set off. . . .

At this very moment, he reflected, from a dozen diverse outposts of the vast and clamorous metropolis, his students, too, were wending their way to the school to which they came with such eagerness and from which they expected so much. Miss Mitnick was probably subjecting her homework to yet another revision on the Fourteenth Street bus. (What a salutary student Miss Mitnick was!) Peter Studniczka was no doubt on the BMT, mumbling over his battered copy of *1,000 Words Commonly Misspelled.* (Sometimes Mr. Parkhill wondered whether Mr. Studniczka was as much influenced by the columns in which the words were spelled right as he was by the columns in which they were spelled wrong.) Miss Tarnova was most likely thinking up Open Questions on the Lexington Avenue subway as she brushed her long eyelashes with mascara. (Mr. Parkhill often wished Miss Tarnova would pay as much attention to her conjugations as she did to her cosmetics.) Mr. C. J. Fledermann was no doubt flexing his reflexes by drilling himself on irregular verbs. Miss Lola Lopez had no doubt attended Mass by now, and Nathan P. Nathan—Mr. Parkhill wondered what gremlins accounted for that young man's tireless jubilations, or his habit of winking, or his compulsion to augment words, from time to time, by endowing them with superfluous syllables.

What interesting, what unusual persons his students were! They came from a score of lands and cultures. He had spent almost nine years now introducing immigrants to the mysteries of English. Nine years. . . . Why, over three hundred students must have sat before him in that time. Some he remembered quite vividly, others—scarcely at all. Some had been swift to learn, others so slow, even obtuse. Some students were B.K. and some were A.K. . . .

Mr. Parkhill stopped dead in his tracks, frowning. Why on *earth* was he falling into that exasperating habit again? It was absurd, perfectly absurd! Why could he not shake it off, once and for all? *Qui docet* certainly should *discet*.

The bizarre initialing had begun almost two weeks ago, when he had awakened from a dream with a pounding heart and drenched with perspiration. (Even when he played squash, Mr. Parkhill rarely became *drenched* with perspiration.) And the dream had recurred, to his dismay, at least five times.

There was nothing especially complicated about the dream; it contained no esoteric symbols (Mr. Parkhill had reread Freud carefully) such as appear in the dreams of even the least neurotic among us. It certainly contained nothing (if you ignored the ladder) which could by the most fanciful stretch of the imagination be called "erotic"

38

or even "libidinal." No. It was just a plain, run-of-the-mill dream. This was what psychiatrists called its "manifest content":

A huge crowd was gathered before the school building, which stood freshly painted, sparkling with untrue radiance and bedecked with gay flags and carnival banners. Some sort of ceremony was taking place. In one version of the dream, Mr. Leland Robinson, principal of the A.N.P.S.A., was addressing the throng; in another, the Chief Justice of the United States, dressed in majestic, if incongruous, regalia (curled-locks wig, white ruff, a voluminous scarlet robe) was delivering the oration; and several times it had been none other than the Secretary-General of the United Nations himself who held the crowd in the dream spellbound.

But it was not that part of the dream that always tore Mr. Parkhill's sleep asunder. The part from which Mr. Parkhill regularly awakened, throat parched and temples hammering, the only part of the dream, indeed, that repeated itself in identical form no matter *who* was delivering the main oration, occurred when the festivities suddenly stopped, a hush gripped the multitude, and Mr. Parkhill found himself the target of all eyes. The entire faculty and student body of the A.N.P.S.A. were staring at him in silent accusation—until (for reasons he could never make out) he began to climb a gigantic ladder in excruciating slow motion. He mounted the rungs with moanings, for a bronze plaque was strapped to his back. The ladder seemed a hundred stories high, even though it rested just above the entrance to the school. What Mr. Parkhill seemed driven to do, from that awful ladder, was hang the bronze plaque on a gigantic hook above the doorway. Engraved on the plaque in Gothic, golden letters was this legend:

AMERICAN NIGHT PREPARATORY SCHOOL
FOR ADULTS
Founded 1910
b. 35 years B.K.
d. "?" years A.K.

That "?" always blazed like a neon sign, the ? in bright red and the " " in blue. The A.K., however, was outlined in green.

A horn, howling into his very eardrum, caused Mr. Parkhill to jump back to the curb just as a truck whooshed by his nose and a hoarse voice implored God to strike him dead. Mr. Parkhill apologized to the vacant air. The traffic light, which he had utterly forgotten to observe, was indubitably red. Or had he mistaken the red of the light for the red of the "?"?! He felt ashamed of himself.

He replaced the briefcase that had slipped to his knees, stepped back up the curb, and waited for the light to change. It changed to green, of course; Mr. Parkhill swiftly crossed the street.

"B.K." . . . "A.K." Oh, he knew what those cryptic notations signified! They stood for "Before Kaplan" and "After Kaplan." In fact, that was the key to the whole dream, which simply converted into symbolic form a thought that must have been churning and churning, unresolved, below Mr. Parkhill's consciousness: *viz.*, that the American Night Preparatory School for Adults, which actually had been founded a good many years before Mr. Kaplan ever entered its doors, was doomed to survive only "?" years after Mr. Kaplan left them. Left? That was just the point. Would Mr. Kaplan ever leave?

The question had haunted Mr. Parkhill long before he had been hounded by that disquieting dream. For he did not see how he could, in conscience, promote Mr. Kaplan to Miss Higby's grade (only last week Mr. Kaplan had said that the plural of "sandwich" is "delicatessen"), and Mr.

40

Parkhill could not bring himself to advise Mr. Kaplan, as he was often tempted, to transfer to some other night school where he might perhaps be happier.

The undeniable fact was that there was no other night school in which Hyman Kaplan could possibly be happier: Mr. Parkhill might be happier; Miss Higby might be happier; at least half of his colleagues in the beginners' grade would surely be *much* happier. But Mr. Kaplan? That buoyant scholar displayed the strongest conceivable affection, an affection bordering on idolatry, for his alma mater.

That was another sticky point: the A.N.P.S.A. could not possibly be the alma mater of one who had never been graduated from it; yet Mr. Kaplan had a way of acting as if it already was.

And that was yet another of the baffling traits which made Mr. Kaplan so difficult to contend with: his cavalier attitude to reality, which he seemed to think he could alter to suit himself. How else could one characterize a man who identified the most famous Strauss waltz as "The Blue Daniel"? Or who, recounting the tale of the cloak spread in the mud before Queen Elizabeth the First, had credited the gallantry to "Sir Walter Reilly"?

Every way Mr. Parkhill turned, he seemed to sink deeper and deeper into the Kaplan morass. For if Mr. Kaplan could not be promoted, or lured away to greener pastures, what *could* Mr. Parkhill do about him? Sometimes Mr. Parkhill wondered if Mr. Kaplan was deliberately trying to remain in the beginners' grade for the rest of his (i.e., Mr. Parkhill's) life. This thought had begun to worry Mr. Parkhill so much that he had brought it up at the last faculty meeting.

Right after Miss Schnepfe had reminded the faculty that each teacher was responsible for snapping off the lights before leaving the classroom, and that the sofa in the faculty lounge had broken another spring and might have to be sent out for repairs, Mr. Robinson asked if there were any other problems which ought to be brought to his attention. "Any problems," he beamed. "As you know, I do not believe in hampering discussion with rigid agendas!"

Mrs. O'Hallohan had raised the perennial problem of ventilation. On very cold nights, classrooms were stifling and classes disturbed by the clanging of radiators; and on very hot nights, the fans near the ceiling did little to relieve the teachers' discomfort or the students' torpor.

Mr. Robinson's face clouded. He said he would speak severely to Mr. Janowitz, the school's temperamental "custodian."

Miss Melanie Pflaum then raised the problem of the chairs. Was the budget really so sparse that *some* of the one-armed oak relics could not at last be replaced by wider, less rickety seats?

"The blackboards," cut in Mr. Krout, "are far worthier supplicants than the chairs!" Why, half the slates in Mr. Krout's room were so thinned by use and glazed by erasings that they now repelled chalk—"the way Moslems reject pork!" (Mr. Krout certainly had a way with similes.)

Mr. Robinson made a wigwam of his hands as he mulled these complaints over, then told Miss Pflaum that the chairs could more sensibly be reglued than replaced, and Mr. Krout that if he used the blackboards which did not repel chalk *before* he assigned students to the slates which did, he would be surprised by how much he would decrease the wear and tear on the latter and "equalize, so to speak," the condition of the former. "There is a lot of life left in those old boards!" Mr. Robinson exclaimed. "Just transfer some of the workload to the new." (Mr. Robinson meant "the less-used"; there were no new blackboards in Mr. Krout's room, nor in any other.)

Miss Higby asked whether officials of the city's Board of

42

Education (*or* the State Department of Education) had yet indicated whether they would accredit the A.N.P.S.A. Mr. Robinson firmly asked everyone to be stout in faith as long as the application was pending. (It had been pending for forty-six months.)

At this point, the colloquium flagging, Mr. Robinson turned to Mr. Parkhill. "Is there not some problem *you* wish to share with us, Parkhill?"

What Mr. Parkhill wished was that he had not replied so quickly, considering how his question would sound to someone like Mr. Robinson: "Sir, what is the school's policy toward a student who may—er—never be qualified for promotion to a higher grade?"

He would never forget the ooze of ice that froze Mr. Robinson's features. (Few knew that under Mr. Robinson's confident façade seethed emotions that led men to end up as what Mr. Kaplan called "a nervous rag.") "Parkhill," Mr. Robinson steelily murmured, "we may all profit from the ancient adage: *'Presto maturo, presto marcio?!'* Yes: 'The sooner ripe, the sooner rotten!' That applies to pupils no less than fruit! . . . I, for one, never give up hope for slow learners—for *any* slow learner. To my humble way of thinking: better several fruitful semesters in the same grade than one barren promotion to the next!"

That had certainly been a memorable answer, but it left Mr. Parkhill exactly where he had been before: What could be done about Hyman Kaplan? The man simply refused to learn. No, no, Mr. Parkhill promptly corrected himself. It was not that Mr. Kaplan refused to learn; what Mr. Kaplan refused to do was *conform.* That was an entirely different matter. Mr. Parkhill could get Mr. Kaplan to understand a rule—of grammar or spelling or punctuation; what he did not seem able to do was get Mr. Kaplan to *agree* with it. Somewhere, somehow, Hyman Kaplan had gotten it into his head that to bend the knee to custom

43

was a hairsbreadth from bending the neck to slavery. (To Mr. Kaplan, the plural of "pie" was "pious.")

Nor was that all which impeded Mr. Kaplan's progress. The laws of English, after all, have developed century after century, like the common law; and like the common law, they gain in authority precisely from the fact that men go on observing them down the countless years. But Mr. Kaplan was not in the slightest impressed by precedent. He seemed to take the position that every rule of grammar, every canon of syntax, every convention of usage, no matter how ancient or formidable, had to prove its case anew. He seemed to want the whole English language to start from scratch. It had taken considerable persuasion on Mr. Parkhill's part, for instance, to convince Mr. Kaplan that there is no feminine form of "ghost." For Mr. Kaplan argued, not without a certain merit, that since a feminine host is a "hostess," a feminine ghost should be a "ghostess."

It was most trying. Mr. Parkhill was beginning to think that the secret to Mr. Kaplan's uniqueness lay in the fact that whereas all the other students came to school in order to be instructed, Mr. Kaplan came in order to be consulted.

Not that the man was an obstreperous pupil. On the contrary. Not one of Mr. Parkhill's three hundred abecedarians (that was what Mr. Robinson liked to call students) had ever been more cooperative, more enthusiastic, more athirst and aflame for knowledge. The trouble was that Mr. Kaplan was so enthusiastic, so athirst and aflame for knowledge that he converted the classroom into a courtroom—a courtroom, moreover, in which the English language was forced to take the stand as defendant. Indeed, Mr. Kaplan sometimes acted as if English had to justify its every rule under his anointed cross-examination.

How else could one describe a situation in which Mr. Kaplan maintained that if a pronoun is a word used in

44

place of a noun, a proverb is a pronoun used in place of a verb? It was preposterous, of course; yet when Mr. Parkhill had challenged Mr. Kaplan to give the class *one single example* of a pronoun used in place of a verb, Mr. Kaplan, transported by that elation which possessed him *in statu pupillari,* beamed, "I'll give t'ree exemples. Soppoze you are on vacation, an' somebody esks: 'Who vants to go for a svim?' T'ree pipple enswer: 'I!' 'Me!' 'You!' All pronons. No voibs." (Mr. Olansky had almost had a stroke that night.)

Surely a student could not be permitted to go on the way Mr. Kaplan did, changing the tongue of Keats and Swift and Trollope to suit himself. But if a pupil refused to accept authority, the testimony of experts, the awesome weight of precedent, to what higher court could his preceptor possibly appeal? Ay, there was the rub. (Mr. Kaplan believed that modern cities consist of streets, boulevards, and revenues.)

Mind you, Mr. Parkhill reminded himself, Mr. Kaplan had never denied that English had rules—good, even admirable, rules. What he would not accept, apparently, was that the rules applied to *him.* Mr. Kaplan had a way of getting Mr. Parkhill to submit each rule to the test of "rizzon," and Mr. Parkhill was beginning to face the awful suspicion that he was no match for a man who operated with rules of reason entirely his own. Only a man with rules of reason entirely his own would have the audacity to give the opposite of "height" as "lowth," or the plural of "woman" as "married." Sometimes Mr. Parkhill thought Mr. Kaplan would never find peace until he had invented a language all his own.

In trying to grope his way through the fog of his dilemma, Mr. Parkhill had even taken Miss Higby into his confidence. "Miss Higby," he had said during a recess, "it might just be that one of my students is a—well, a kind of genius."

"Genius?" echoed Miss Higby.

"Y-yes. I mean, he pays close attention, never fails to do his homework, volunteers every time we have Open Questions or General Discussion, and yet—well—I mean . . ." Mr. Parkhill illustrated his quandary by being unable to describe it.

"And *that* makes you think he's a 'genius'?"

"No," protested Mr. Parkhill. "What I'm trying to say is that he—well, he seems to take the position that since he raises no objection to our rules, why should we object to—er—his?"

Miss Higby had made a sort of gurgling noise. "I think we're going to get an extra day of vacation this semester!" She hurried to her room.

That remark had made Mr. Parkhill quite cross. It was not at all a matter of an extra day of vacation, this semester or any other. Vacation had nothing to do with it. The trouble with Miss Higby was that, like Mr. Robinson, she could not see the forest for the trees; worse, people like that could not see the *trees* because they were so preoccupied with the forest. They refused to face facts.

They refused to face facts, Mr. Parkhill felt, just as Mr. Kaplan refused to abide by conventions. Still, that did not absolve the American Night Preparatory School for Adults of its responsibility; it only added to its burdens.

What Mr. Parkhill finally concluded was that if Mr. Kaplan refused to enter their universe, they would have to enter his. Mr. Parkhill no longer doubted that Mr. Kaplan did live and think in a universe all his own. That would explain how he had come to define "diameter" as a machine that counts dimes, or named the waterway which connects the Atlantic and Pacific "the Panama Kennel."

Mr. Parkhill passed his hand across his brow. He wondered if it might not be best to think of Mr. Kaplan not as a pupil but as some sort of cosmic force, a reckless, independent star that swam through the heavens in its own unpredictable orbit. (After all, Mr. Kaplan referred to England's titan of science, codifier of the laws of gravity, as "Isaac Newman.")

Mr. Kaplan was simply *sui generis*. Perhaps that was why he so often responded with delight, rather than despair, when Mr. Parkhill corrected him. It had taken Mr. Parkhill a long time to discover that Mr. Kaplan's smile signified not agreement but consolation. Where all the other students sank into gloom upon committing an error, Mr. Kaplan shot into the clouds from which to celebrate his originality. . . .

Ahead loomed the school building. Tonight, bathed in gossamer moonbeams, it took on a ghostly grandeur.

Mr. Parkhill removed his hat as he went up the worn stone steps. Just as he opened the door, a voice behind him sang out, "Goot ivnink, Mr. Pockheel!"

He did not have to think or turn to know whose voice that was. No one else pronounced his name quite that way, or infused a routine salutation with the timbre of Archimedes crying "Eureka!"

"Vhat's a madder? You not fillink Hau Kay?"

"I beg your pardon?"

"You vere lookink so fonny on de school."

Mr. Parkhill caught a glimpse of Mr. Kaplan's bright, benign mien, beclouded, for a moment, with solicitude.

"It's nothing," said Mr. Parkhill hastily. "Nothing at all."

But he knew that he *had* been "lookink fonny on de school." He could have sworn that for one demented moment he had seen, twinkling over the entrance:

b. 25 years B.K.
d. "?" years A.K.

They entered the temple together.

47

4

MR. K·A·P·L·A·N CONQUERS AN AD

It was with a feeling of genuine usefulness that Mr. Park-hill announced: "Your homework assignment, class, will be of special interest!" He smiled.

Mr. Parkhill found himself smiling a great deal lately—not because he was a smiling type (on the contrary, he was an earnest, unsmiling type), and not because he actually felt like smiling. He smiled because he knew how much his students appreciated it. It soothed their anxieties; it stiffened their confidence; it definitely shored up their morale. He could not help but see how swiftly the class reacted to the subtlest variation of his moods—elated by his approval, depressed by his concern, crushed by his displeasure.

"The assignment," he continued, the smile cemented to his lips, "is a practical exercise which you will be able to put to—er—practical use."

At the first "practical" the entire congregation had sat up; at the second, they leaned forward. If there was any-thing they hungered for, it was to wring utility from a heartless tongue.

"Take an advertisement out of a newspaper—any adver-tisement, for a job, an automobile, a vacuum cleaner, any advertisement at all—and answer it!" Mr. Parkhill's smile congealed; to his surprise, not joy but unease swept the faces before him.

"Answer an *att?*" someone quavered.

"In *English?*" someone queried.

"*Me?!*" quaked Mrs. Yanoff, her black dress reinforcing her pessimism.

"Now, now," Mr. Parkhill reassured them, "the assignment is not hard. After all, you have all seen the 'Help Wanted' or 'For Sale' columns in newspapers." He replaced his ailing smile with a fresh edition. "Well, over this next weekend, simply look through a newspaper, select an ad, *any* ad that interests you, and—just answer it!"

Groans of uncertainty swelled into alarums of dismay, climaxed by an "Oy!" of premature defeat. Mrs. Moskowitz was already fanning herself with her notebook.

"Remember," Mr. Parkhill quickly added, "we have already had exercises in writing letters, both personal and business. Let's say this homework involves simply *another* exercise in letter writing!"

"Ufcawss! Plain an' tsimple!" That was Hyman Kaplan, and for once Mr. Parkhill felt grateful to that dauntless spirit.

"Are there any questions?"

Minnie Pilpul raised her left hand. (Actually, Mrs. Pilpul, who was left-handed, only elevated her thumb.) "Could you be so kind to give a for instance?"

"I beg your pardon?"

"She means be so kind and give an *example*," explained Miss Mitnick.

"Ha!" scoffed Mr. Kaplan. "Who nidds more exemples? Mr. Pockheel axplained it poifick! 'Halp vanted.' 'For Sale.' Iven a baby could unnistand!" He scowled at the widow Pilpul for flinching before what any infant could understand, and sniffed at Miss Mitnick for giving aid and comfort to a backslider.

"I only t-tried to help," Miss Mitnick stammered.

"An' *I*," said Mr. Kaplan, "don nidd exemples of exemples!"

"Stop!" boomed Reuben Olansky, glaring at Mr. Studniczka, who had not uttered a sound. "Let *once* the class not be an all-for-free!"

"It's 'free-for-all,'" remarked Mr. Parkhill.

"Ha!" exulted Mr. Kaplan. "Olansky ken't iven *object* corract!"

"Keplan," glowered Mr. Blattberg, "give a rest your tongue!"

"Tonight will be a three-rink circus!" laughed Nathan P. Nathan.

"Gentlemen," said Mr. Parkhill hastily. "Mrs. Pilpul's request is quite in order; I shall be glad to offer several more—er—specific examples." The Mitnick-Olansky-Blattberg patrol basked in Mr. Parkhill's favor. "You may, for instance, answer an ad that offers to rent a room, or sell a radio, or—or—" To his annoyance, Mr. Parkhill's mind went blank—totally, exasperatingly blank. He scoured the cellars of memory for those images, those classified images, he knew must be stored there by the thousands. "Or a free dancing lesson!"

It was not, alas, an ideal example.

"*Dencing* lessons?" gasped Mrs. Moskowitz. "At my age who takes from Arthur Murphy?"

"Arthur Murray. . . ."

"It's only *vun* exemple!" blurted Mr. Kaplan. "Mr. Pockheel also offert a room to rant!"

"My flet has already four rooms, so who needs—"

"So don't rant a room! Buy a car!"

"Class—"

"A car?" bristled Mr. Hruska. "Who affords?"

"Buy it *sacond-hend!*"

"Mr. Kap—"

"An exemple isn't a pair hencuffs!" retorted Mr. Kaplan. "Hruska, you got to use imegination!"

"I don't understand ads," sulked Lola Lopez. "They use *leetle* words wheech—"

"Those," said Mr. Parkhill at once, "are *abbreviations*. And, as a matter of fact, working with them might turn out to be one of the most useful features of the assignment! You will have the whole weekend—"

"I hate dosa 'brevyations'!" declared Lucca Barbella.

Mr. Kaplan hurled a "Ha!" at shameless Barbella. "Abbrevyations didn't bodder Ban Frenklin or J. P. Morton."

"They dida not answer ads!" cracked Rome's native son.

"Dey vould thank Gott for de *chence!* To find a varm room mit a roof over deir had! To go by car, instad on tired fit—"

"Class—"

"Stop!" roared Reuben Olansky, groping through an outrage that only reblurred his vision. "Why do you drag in by his shoes J. B. Moran? And where did Benjam Franklin use abbreviations?"

"That's right!"

"Vhere?"

"Give even one case!"

"Keplen," rejoined Mr. Kaplan with hauteur, "is prezanting exemples, not takink cross-exemination!"

Mr. Pinsky cried "Pssh!" and slapped his cheek.

Mr. Olansky smote his forehead, howling.

"That will be enough, class," said Mr. Parkhill crossly. "There are many *simple* ads from which you may choose. I suggest you copy the advertisement you decide to answer, or—better yet, clip it out of the paper! Bring it to class with your letter. Then, I am quite sure—"

Before he could tell them what he was quite sure of, Mr. Kaplan's contempt boiled over. "Vhat kind students ve got in cless enyhow? Did Mr. Pockheel bag us on banded knees to comm to school? Did he sand ot ingraved invitations? Did de Prazident sign a law dat averybody got to enswer an ed or go to jail?"

The list of particulars enraged the anti-Kaplan cabal, who raised an uproar, which triggered deafening defenses from Kaplan's comrades. Mr. Pinsky accused Miss Lopez of jeopardizing the class's morale by questioning Mr. Parkhill's judgment; Olaf Umea fumed that Mr. Pinsky was Mr. Kaplan's spineless lackey. Miss Kipnis declaimed that Mr. Kaplan was an adornment to the grade and a model for the brave; Miss Tarnova moped that "this mon" was a wolf in cat's clothing. Isaac Nussbaum tried to mollify both legions by quoting Isaiah, but the beating of swords into ploughshares was lost in the bellow of C. J. Fledermann excoriating those "stoogies" who blindly followed where e'er mad Kaplan led. This prompted Mrs. Shimmelfarb to scourge Christian Fledermann for attacking the pygmies on the sidelines instead of confronting the champion himself on the field of honor. Nathan P. Nathan was in seventh heaven, his laughter so potent that it wakened Mr. Trabish from his slumbers.

"Class! Class!" Mr. Parkhill kept protesting. "We *can*not go on this way! Order. Please—everyone—compose yourselves!"

In the imposed composure which followed, Miss Goldberg reached for a peppermint, Miss Lopez crossed herself, and Stanislaus Wilkomirski fired one patriotic shot of parting: "America is free country!"

"Amarica," crooned Hyman Kaplan, "did not gat freedom from pipple who are afraid to enswer an ed!"

But all that was over and done with. It was the following Monday night. Peace—and work—enveloped the scholars, who had crammed the blackboards with their homework.

The assignment was turning out to be more successful than Mr. Parkhill had dared hope. Miss Kipnis opened the evening with a rather effective, if repetitious, reply to an advertisement of the Bell Telephone Company:

Dear Telephone—

Your ad says you want young women. I am young woman.

You print "salary good." Good.

You want girls to come to office Wed. 9–1. I will come to office Wed. 9–1.

Happily yours,

Clara (Cookie) Kipnis, "Miss"

The diagnosis of this offering had been both brisk and productive: Mr. Milas Wodjik challenged the propriety of "Dear Telephone," and Mr. Tomas Wodjik promptly added that "Dear Company" would be better. Miss Ziev remarked that placing a "Miss" between quotation marks was both superfluous and misleading (on Miss Ziev's left hand gleamed the new ring with which Mr. Andrassy had repledged eternal devotion). Miss Mitnick suggested that "Happily yours" was not proper in business correspondence and might, besides, give the Bell Telephone System the impression that the applicant was too flighty to be entrusted with "calls from a long distance." Mrs. Pilpul wondered whether it was not more accurate to write "I will come to office *between* 9 and 1," instead of "I will come to office 9–1." "The way *she* wrote," observed the hearty widow, "she will be standing on her lags four hours!"

Mr. Parkhill had congratulated the critics on their acumen.

Mr. Fledermann's letter followed Miss Kipnis's; and C. J. Fledermann, Mr. Parkhill was delighted to see, had shown exceptional bravery in answering a long advertisement from the Bronx Unique Products Agency for "GO-GETTERS!" interested in augmenting their income by selling, on commission, hand-colored portraits of the Pope, which were "guaranteed to sell like hot cakes." Mr. Fledermann's salutation was correct, his text commendable, his final greeting impeccable. His downfall, alas, came *via* an unnecessary postscript:

P.S. I like to sell hot cakes.

Mr. Parkhill went to considerable pains to explain the difference between selling hot cakes and selling *like* hot cakes. Nathan P. Nathan went into a paroxysm.

Not all the students, of course, had reached the laudable levels of a Kipnis or a Fledermann. Mr. Studniczka, for instance, had answered a notice announcing the sale of "Furn., unpainted" by declaring that he was a wizard at removing paint from furnaces. Mrs. Shimmelfarb had unfortunately mistaken "Lab. Tech." for "labor teacher." Miss Atrakian had applied for a position which required "Highest refs." by stating that she heartily approved of any business firm that gave "highest refunds."

And there had been other pitfalls—mares' nests which no one, not even Mr. Parkhill, could possibly have foreseen. Mr. Umea had replied to a notice offering $25 reward for a lost dog with a letter that contained this baffling line:

Send $25.00. I found your college dog.

The class might have gotten entirely out of hand ("What kind dog is smot enough to pess even high school?" "They lost a *dog,* not a student!") had not Mr. Parkhill, in a stroke of inspiration, solved the mystery: Olaf Umea simply had thought "collie" the abbreviation for "college."

Tiny Lola Lopez had drafted an answer to "Wanted: Housekeeper" which cunningly reduced the probability of error to the very bone:

Dear Ad:
I am housekeeper.
L. Lopez

There was not much one could do with that.

Now the last platoon was at the blackboard. Rochelle

54

Goldberg was putting the finishing touches to her précis of qualifications for the post of receptionist for Juno Princess Slips. Mr. Pinsky was completing an epistle to "Zig Zag Zippers, Inc." Miss Olga Tarnova, whose throaty suspirations hinted of a time when spurned lovers had flung themselves off cliffs from Monte Carlo to Murmansk, was addressing a Hindu seer who claimed to have direct entrée to the hereafter:

Ahmed Taj' Chandra
Box 308
Eve. Post

Ah, dear Ahmed—
I saw soulful ad you wrote to help world grow in Secret
Powers. Many nights I sleep awake—

Mr. Parkhill read no further; he *wished* Miss Tarnova would begin to use the definite article, and choose less exotic material.

The letter to Miss Tarnova's right was—Mr. Kaplan's. There could not be the slightest doubt that it was Mr. Kaplan's, for on the board was printed:

ANSWERING AN AD
by
H*Y*M*A*N K*A*P*L*A*N

The author stood poised before his handiwork as if he were Leonardo—one hand holding his notebook as if it were a palette, the other wielding the chalk as if it were a brush, examining his masterpiece with narrowed eyes and a lilting hum of approbation, taking a step back or a lunge forward as the divine afflatus moved him. Mr. Parkhill sighed. How Mr. Kaplan loved a blackboard: to him the slate was no lifeless surface on which to record his homework; to him it was a golden road to posterity.

As Miss Tarnova signed her name to her letter with a

flourish, the bracelets on her wrist tinkling, the master, jarred out of communion with the Muses, scowled, "Tell me, Tarnova, vhich symphony of Mozart's you playink: de foist or de lest?"

Miss Tarnova did not deign response; she flared her fine nostrils and glided back to her seat like a Grand Duchess spurning a *moujik*.

"Please finish," Mr. Parkhill quickly called. "Take your seats. . . . We shall begin with—Miss Goldberg."

It was a good choice: Miss Goldberg had outdone herself. Her application for the post of receptionist at Juno Princess Slips was terse and telling. The only question anyone raised was whether "Dear Madam" might not be more fitting than "Dear Gentlemen" for "someone in princess slips."

Mr. Pinsky's letter to Zig Zag Zippers, Inc., ran into stormier weather. Mr. Pinsky had for some reason composed his entire communication in capitals:

HELLO.
I SAW YOUR AD FOR BUS OPERATOR
I ACCEPT $25,000, SO—

"Holy smoky!" Mr. Nussbaum, ever the cantor, exclaimed before the floor was even thrown open for discussion. "That is a telegram, not a letter!"

"Is this night school or Western Union?" demanded Mr. Blattberg.

"It's a picnic," chortled Mr. Nathan.

Mr. Kaplan dashed to aid his aide-de-camp. "Telegrams get rizzolts! Congradulation, Pinsky!"

Mr. Olansky raised his hand, glaring at Miss Atrakian, whom he mistook for Mr. Pinsky, and in caustic vocables inquired how any business in its right mind could offer twenty-five thousand dollars to a bus driver. "Not even in Tel Aviv!"

The challenge did not faze Sam Pinsky, who handed Mr.

56

Parkhill the clipping in question. The twenty-five thousand dollars was there, all right, but it had been requested, not offered. When Mr. Parkhill explained that "Bus. opp." means "Business opportunity," not "Bus operator," Mr. Pinsky looked badly shaken.

"Don't take it hod," Mr. Kaplan murmured.

"Charge admission!" gurgled Mr. Nathan.

"Gentlemen. . . . The next letter . . ."

Miss Tarnova read her letter, one hand at her throat. "Ah, dear Ahmed," she intoned, "I saw soulful ad you wrote, to help world grow in Secret Power. . . ." (Mr. Trabish yawned; the lure of the East cast no spell on Oscar Trabish, who had trouble staying awake during Open Questions, much less attuning his soul to the supernatural.) "Many nights I sleep awake—"

"You slip avake?" cried Mr. Kaplan. "Ha! Maybe you also sit stendink op?"

Olga Tarnova sniffed her perfumed kerchief in olfactory rebuff. As soon as her dulcet rendition ended, Mr. Parkhill said, "That is a most *interesting* letter. There are—a few mistakes, but on the whole you have improved in every way." She certainly *had* improved. (Miss Tarnova's previous recitation was called: "Leopold Stokowski, Don't Butcher Tchaikovsky!") "Comments, class?"

Mr. Wilkomirski recommended a comma after the unpunctuated salutation. Lola Lopez tried to persuade Miss Tarnova to *lie* awake instead of sleeping awake. Mr. Hruska asked, "Why 'Dear Ahmed'? Is not more polite 'Mister Chandra'?"

Miss Mitnick addressed herself to Miss Tarnova's final greeting, which virtually leaped from the blackboard:

I remain,
A soul-mat

Olga ("Panjura") Tarnova

"I'm sure," Miss Mitnick said earnestly, "Miss Tarnova meant to put 'e' on the end of 'mat.'"

"Da, da," moaned the soulful diva.

"Very good." Mr. Parkhill started to convert the "mat" of Miss Tarnova's soul into its "mate," when Mr. Kaplan cut in sternly: "Vhat's all of a sodden dis 'Penjura'? Is dat a name or a game?!"

"To Ahmed I am 'Ponjura'!" flared Miss Tarnova. "In Hindu spirit world we all take new names!"

"For dat you don't have to go to Hindus. *Prisons* are pecked full of pipple who used fake names."

"Pssh!" admiring Pinsky's slap on the cheek rang out.

"Koplon, where is your *soul?!*" shouted Miss Tarnova.

"Naxt to my hills," said Mr. Kaplan.

"Bodzhe moi!" cursed the "Rossian."

Nathan P. Nathan was holding his sides.

"Next! Next!" Mr. Parkhill rapped a rattling tattoo with his pointer. He shot a quick glance at the clock. Only nine minutes remained. (How he had hoped there were less.) The final letter was Mr. Kaplan's.

The room stirred like a field of wheat before a heralding wind as Hyman Kaplan rose. That careless smile, that shooting of the cuffs, that benevolent gleam to those about to share in impending revelation—then Hyman Kaplan grasped his lapels in the manner of Disraeli, and read: "'Enswerink an Ed, by Hyman Keplen.'"

Mr. Parkhill lowered himself into his chair.

Mr. Kaplan read his text with matchless fervor:

Box 701
Daily New
New York

Dear Box,
   One day was Hyman Kaplan home, feeling his blues, thinking "What is world coming to? No body happy, people worryd, we live on a vulcano."

"How a man can find peace?" asked Hyman Kaplan. How a man can escape this jongle? No way.

No way? *Stop, Hyman Kaplan!* Look. Listen. Read what is here in the paper in front your 2 eyes! A wonderful ad! What it says? This it says—

"Man with ambition. Must have ideas, imag., init., drive. Salary no object. Box 701."

O.K. Box 701, look no more! I am that man.

1. "Ideas" I have plenty
2. "Imag." I can imagine anything
3. "Init." My initials are H. K.
4. "Drive." I don't—but willing to learn.
        Y.T.

                H*Y*M*A*N K*A*P*L*A*N

Before Mr. Kaplan could finish his name, the wolves were baying at the moon.

"What is that 'Dear Box'?" glared Mr. Olansky.

"Important eds give only a 'Box,'" said Mr. Kaplan.

"Should be 'Dear *sir,*'" stammered Miss Mitnick. "Not 'Dear B-box!'"

"How do you know is only vun boss in dat box?" returned Mr. Kaplan.

"You were feeling your 'blue*s*'?" blustered Mr. Blattberg. "Should be singular—'blue'!"

"I falt *vary* blue, so I made plural."

"'Daily *New*' should be 'Daily *News*'!" protested C. J. Fledermann.

"Since vhen is vun copy plural?" sniped Mr. Kaplan, reversing his field.

Now the emendations came fast and furious.

"'No body' should be 'nobody,'" trilled Lola Lopez.

"Excellent," said Mr. Parkhill.

"That word 'drive' in ads means energy," objected Miss Atrakian, "not car-driving."

"Good!"

"What is that bandaged-op 'Y.T.'? Is Koplan too *weak* to

write out 'Yours truly'?" Mr. Olansky was so offended that he resorted to maximal insult: deliberately turning his chair so that he could turn his back on his *bête noir*.

The class swarmed across Mr. Kaplan's mistakes, not heeding Mr. Parkhill's anxious interventions, not pausing to let Mr. Kaplan reply. Had they been less drunk from the taste of blood, they would have noticed that Mr. Kaplan was not even trying to respond. He was the picture of aplomb. But such courageous forbearance was too much for the faithful, who rallied to his banner.

"Keplen, *say* something!" begged steadfast Pinsky.

"Mr. Kaplan, *answer*," pleaded loyal Gidwitz.

"Go on, Mr. Edison," sneered Mr. Olansky to the rear wall. "Make a miracle!"

"Class . . ." called Mr. Parkhill. "We *must* speak one at a time! Those who wish to comment on Mr. Kaplan's letter —please wait to be recognized. . . . Miss Mitnick."

"I see five more mistakes," announced Miss Mitnick. "At least."

"Fife mistakes!" chortled Mrs. Moskowitz.

"At *least*," concurred C. J. Fledermann.

The mistakes Rose Mitnick saw and named and pinned to the mat of analysis were but the beginning. Other voices sought Mr. Parkhill's sanction; other scholars leaped into the fray. The errata of Hyman Kaplan unrolled on a seemingly endless scroll.

Yet, nothing ruffled the man's sangfroid. To every blunder pinpointed, every sarcastic suggestion or sardonic change, Mr. Kaplan made no demurrer. Even the laughter of Nathan P. Nathan drew no riposte from Mr. Kaplan— save once, when he smiled with mystifying kindliness, "I see you now realize aducation can be a plashure, boychik."

Mr. Parkhill began to feel alarmed. He was placing so many corrections on the board that his wrist was beginning to ache; yet Mr. Kaplan offered not a word of defense.

60

He simply stood there, lofty, almost courtly, neither chastened nor abashed. Mr. Parkhill's scalp began to prickle. He thought he caught a gleam in Mr. Kaplan's eyes.

The longer Mr. Kaplan met criticism with such nobility, and rectification with such grace, the more Mr. Parkhill fought off a sense of panic. He could understand fortitude under fire. He was quite familiar with Mr. Kaplan's invulnerability to humiliation. But he could not help wondering when and how that virtuoso of escape would remain unscathed. Experience warned Mr. Parkhill that perhaps Mr. Kaplan's surprising sufferance was only camouflage for some unsprung trap.

The hands of the clock crawled to 9:58. Only two minutes remained, almost nothing left to correct, when Miss Mitnick raised her hand once more. "Why does Mr. Kaplan give his initials? Doesn't the abbreviation 'i-n-i-t' mean 'initia*tive*'?"

"Of course!" said Mr. Parkhill. (He had not thought anyone would catch that.) " 'Initia*tive,*' Mr. Kaplan."

Mr. Kaplan nodded politely. "But de ed *I* enswered vanted my initials."

Mr. Parkhill studied his chalk cautiously. "Mr. Kaplan, there is hardly any—uh—room for difference about what 'i-n-i-t' means."

"In general, or in dis poticular ed?"

"Koplan, stop sneaking!" Mr. Olansky gloated to the ceiling.

"Admit you are wrong!" shouted one of the Wodjiks.

"Give an *inch!*" pleaded Bessie Shimmelfarb. *"Once* only, give an *inch."*

Hyman Kaplan spurned geometric appeasement.

"Mr. Kaplan," said Mr. Parkhill suddenly, "suppose we settle the point by referring to the text of the advertisement you answered."

"It's on de board."

"Your *reply* to the ad is on the board," said Mr. Parkhill frigidly. "I asked for the—actual ad."

"Onfortunately," said Hyman Kaplan, "dere is no ectual ed."

"Hanh?" cried Mr. Olansky, wheeling around.

"A trick!" charged Mr. Blattberg.

"Tropped, tropped!" rejoiced Miss Tarnova.

A monstrous—an unbelievable—truth began to dawn on Mr. Parkhill. "Mr. Kaplan, are you telling us that *you made up the ad?"*

"Soitinly," said Mr. Kaplan.

"No!" howled Reuben Olansky.

"Mein Gott!" moaned Isaac Nussbaum.

"Who can beat Kaplan?!" cheered Mr. Pinsky.

Mr. Parkhill put his chalk down without a word. He made no effort to calm the furor of the hoodwinked which exploded around him. Mr. Kaplan, never content with reality as he found it, had simply composed his own ad.

Perhaps it was his need to be different. Perhaps it was his need to reconstruct life to suit his heart's desire. And perhaps, Mr. Parkhill shuddered, the perverse genius that governed Hyman Kaplan had known all along that there was no higher authority on earth for the meaning of "init." than the man who had placed that abbreviation in his own ad.

5

THE G·O·O·D SAMARITAN

"Yos, it was romonteek, but trogic. How Nicolai Ilyich soffered! The day and the night, the week ofter the week, dear Babushka prayed—"

"Miss Tarnova," Mr. Parkhill interrupted gently, "in English, we say 'day and night,' not *the* day and *the* night.' Watch those definite articles. . . ."

Olga Tarnova's languorous lashes fluttered. *"Da.* Dear Babushka went to chorch to pray, to find the hope for cure—"

Mr. Parkhill cleared his throat apologetically. "I'm afraid it's 'hope,' not *'the* hope,' and *'a* cure,' not *'cure.'* You use the definite article when it is not required, and omit it when it is."

Miss Tarnova's ululations testified to a confusion for which Mr. Parkhill had the utmost sympathy. "So how we con tell when we should use, and when we should not use?!"

"That's a good question." Mr. Parkhill hefted his chalk thoughtfully. "The articles in English may be definite (that is, 'the') or *in*definite (that is, 'a' or 'an'). *'The* boy,' for instance"—swiftly he wrote "the boy" on the board—"is a definite, *particular* boy; but 'a boy' "—the white letters spun under "a boy"—"means any boy—"

"I wos not reciting about boys!" protested Miss Tarnova. "Nicolai Ilyich was soventy-four!"

"Oh. Well, I meant *any* person—boy or man—or any *thing*: 'The clock' is a definite clock, but 'a clock' means any—"

"So my saying *'the* hope' was definite!"

"We-ell," said Mr. Parkhill reluctantly, "when abstract nouns are involved—"

"Ooo," groaned Mrs. Moskowitz.

"—we do not use any article at all."

"Oy!"

"You see, class, abstract nouns are qualities or emotions, like 'hope' or 'fear'—"

"Movvelous!" sang Mr. Kaplan.

"—or 'pity,' 'hate'—"

"I definitely hate some people," flashed Miss Tarnova, "so why is wrong *'the* hate'?"

Mr. Parkhill's palms went moist. "Well, one *can* say 'The hate which—er—Wilbur felt for—' "

"Who's 'Vilbur'?" demanded Mrs. Moskowitz.

" 'Wilbur' was just—an example. Any name would express the point—"

"She hates Koplan!" announced Mr. Olansky.

"Thot's definite!" intoned Miss Tarnova.

Mr. Parkhill studied the door. "Perhaps we should devote our next session to a thorough analysis of articles and abstract nouns." He felt like a coward; but Recitation and Speech had just begun, and the terrain of articles and abstract nouns was strewn with such thorns. . . . "Please return to your recitation, Miss Tarnova. You were saying that—er—Babushka went to church to pray, hoping to find *a* cure. . . ."

Olga Tarnova's dark orbs smouldered. "Also prayed my dear brother, Alexonder Ivanovich, always brave, who said us—"

" *'Told* us.' "

"He *said,* not told!"

Mr. Parkhill wished he did not have to press on. "Then you must say 'said *to us,*' I'm afraid."

Miss Tarnova wrung her hands; she was meant for midnights and mazurkas, not for the heartless stomp of an alien grammar. "Pardone, pardone . . ." She smoothed her tresses with a gesture that would have done credit to Camille. "Alexonder Ivanovich told us all not to worry. So we tried to altogether forget."

"To forgat altogadder!" called Mr. Kaplan.

Miss Tarnova's glare could have started a bonfire. "Whot is wrong now?"

"Tsplit infinitif!"

Mr. Kaplan had, by supreme concentration, memorized three axioms of English syntax, and he clung to them as cosmic verities: "Wrong tanse," "Dobble nagetif," and "Tsplit infinitif!" (It had taken weeks for Mr. Parkhill to convince Mr. Kaplan that it was "tsplit infinitif," not "tsplit infinit*y*"; something about "tsplit infinity" rang bells of recognition in Mr. Kaplan's soul.) Whenever the opportunity arose to use one of these three *obiter dicta,* Mr. Kaplan, ecstatic, seized it. "Tsplit infinitif!"

Miss Tarnova flung out her shapely arms, tinkling all her bracelets, and stamped her foot in fury. "Article—not article—definite, indefinite—splitting finitive! I am Rossian! I say what is in *heart!* English has no soul! *Nitchevo!* I stop!" She flounced to her seat in a perfectly understandable huff.

"Miss Tarnova," Mr. Parkhill said anxiously, "a student does not mean to give offense when he offers—"

It was in vain. Miss Tarnova was imploring others who had fallen before Mr. Kaplan's blade—Miss Mitnick, Mr. Blattberg, myopic Olansky—to waste no time in avenging inequity most foul.

"Won't you come back, Miss Tarnova?" asked Mr. Parkhill earnestly. "Please complete your *most* interesting recitation."

"Other time, maybe. Other time."

"Som odder time," Mr. Kaplan said politely.

A Slavic oath crossed Miss Tarnova's cherry lips.

"My!" said Mr. Kaplan in admiration.

Mr. Parkhill quickly called on Mr. Studniczka.

Peter Ignatius Studniczka trudged to the podium as if to the gallows. It was his début in Recitation and Speech. He stopped at Mr. Parkhill's desk, head bent, cheeks waxen, dripping perspiration.

"Well, Mr. Studniczka!" said Mr. Parkhill cheerfully.

Mr. Studniczka lifted his face. He looked haggard. He was a quiet student who rarely spoke a word in class, or volunteered a comment, and treated homework as if it were poison ivy.

"Er—you may begin," smiled Mr. Parkhill.

The last vestige of life drained out of Peter Studniczka's cheeks. He loosened his tie, then unbuttoned his collar. (*That,* thought Mr. Parkhill, should certainly relieve some of Mr. Studniczka's discomfort.) His eyes went glassy. He opened his mouth—and released a burst of strangling noises: "Lds gntlmns I lak N'Yrk bt nt altime becuz nt lak *wrk* s'hrd. . . ."

The words, if that was what they were, drowned in a gurgling stew. Silence swallowed the gurgle. The class sat stunned. Someone coughed. (Had Nathan P. Nathan come to school that night, he undoubtedly would have laughed, but Mr. Nathan was undoubtedly cheering his head off at Madison Square Garden.)

"A—er—little louder, Mr. Studniczka," said Mr. Parkhill bravely. "And *slower.* Do go on. . . ."

The agonized man fixed his eyes somewhere between the ceiling and the top of Miss Atrakian's head. He parted his lips. His tongue clucked dryly. No words emerged.

Mr. Parkhill kept smiling and nodding and broadcasting enheartenment. Mrs. Yanoff emitted the most friendly bleatings. Miss Goldberg tried to buttress Mr. Studniczka's nerves by the vicarious consumption of a nougat. Mr. Hruska grunted sounds of support. But none of these succoring efforts produced meaningful vocables from Peter Ignatius Studniczka.

Suddenly, Mr. Kaplan leaned far forward and whispered, "Mister, just talk! Ve all on your site!"

Out of the pall that shrouded him, Peter Studniczka searched for the benevolent stranger.

"Is easy! Just talk lod, clear—*netcheral*. . . . Efter all"— the Samaritan smiled—"voice den Tarnova you ken't be!"

Miss Tarnova's impure ejaculation broke the verbal logjam. In one breathless torrent, without the briefest pause or beat or intermittence, Mr. Studniczka bolted into verbosity: "Ladies gantlemans I lak Nev York but not altime. Work too hard but is fine place with good eats and I see nice movie. America is more good as Czestchova, so not sorry I come. Want to marry good lady, cook, wash. Want boy name Dinko, also girl—not care how name. Please."

And like a tornado which had roared into the room and right out, leaving a silence of desolation, Mr. Studniczka, liberated from recitation, stumbled back to his seat.

Mr. Parkhill did not stir for a moment. The class seemed shell-shocked—all but Mr. Kaplan, who was chortling in celebration of the coming-of-age of his ward.

"Er—" Mr. Parkhill spoke up at last (his voice sounded as if he was under water). "Corrections, class . . . ?"

The beginners' grade sat immobilized.

"*No* corrections?" Mr. Parkhill asked lightly. "Surely someone can start us off."

"The speech was so *fast*, who could cetch?" protested Mr. Blattberg.

"*Sí, sí,*" sighed Miss Lopez.

"Hard t'understand," grumbled Milas Wodjik.

"Hard t'understand," grunted Tomas Wodjik.

"Ha!" rang out the sustaining voice of Mr. Kaplan. "Dat spitch vas fromm de hot! A man's emotions you don't see t'rough like gless!"

"He spoke too *fast*," complained Mrs. Pilpul.

"Ve livink in an aitch of speed!" Mr. Kaplan retorted.

"I dida not hear good," complained Lucca Barbella.

"Go to an ear spacialist!" Mr. Kaplan recommended.

"Are there any *specific* corrections?" Mr. Parkhill cut in hopefully.

"Yes!" It was Reuben Olansky. "Even if was too fast, *I* noticed soitin corractions." He cast a smug sneer toward Mr. Pinsky (whom he mistook for his master, Hyman Kaplan), placed his notes within an inch of his nose, and peered through his bifocals. "Was missing lots and lots of 'the' and 'a.' Some verbs were present for past and in the past for present, and futures didn't exist at all! 'Ne*v* York' isn't 'New York' and 'Please' instead 'Thank you' in the last place isn't good in the foist place!"

"Yah! . . . Sure! . . . *Dozens* mistakes!" the pro-Olansky chorus resounded.

Mr. Studniczka stared at his palms.

"Well, class . . ." Mr. Parkhill said slowly, "Mr. Olansky has certainly caught quite a few errors. Perhaps we should—"

An irate voice cleaved the air. "*I* vant to say a few voids!" Mr. Kaplan started for the podium.

"Mr. Kaplan," said Mr. Parkhill, not without alarm, "it is not your *turn.*"

"So pretend it's time for *my* spitch!" Two great strides took Mr. Kaplan to the platform. He buttoned his coat as if buckling on his armor, cast a scythe of scorn across the field of nit-pickers, and exclaimed: "Ladies an' gantleman an' Mr. Pockheel! Vhat's de minnink Jostice?"

The forum stirred uneasily.

"Jostice? J-O-S-T-I-S. Vhat it minns?" Hyman Kaplan ignored the possibility of another's answer. "I'll tell you. Jostice is de finest, de most beauriful idea in history! It's kind! It's sveet! It's nauble! It's liftink op all human beans!" (Mr. Kaplan, indeed, lifted up with the words, dispatching his passion from the increased elevation achieved by raised heels.) "Do *enimals* have Jostice? No! Are—"

"Mr. Kaplan . . ." Mr. Parkhill had just recovered from "human beans." "You must slow down!" It was like asking Demosthenes to put the pebbles back in his mouth.

"—Are *sevedges* havink Jostice? No! Den who got it? Tsivilized pipple!"

" '*Pe*ople,' not '*pip*—' "

"In *dis* room are soitin types who forgat de rizzon ve all came to vunderful U.S.! Vhy? Becawss here are de stritts pasted wit' gold? Ha! Becawss ve vould all gat rich all of a sodden?!" The judicial features clouded. "You might as vell try to ritch de moon wit' a toot-pick!"

"Stop!" howled Reuben Olansky (but what howl can be heard in a hurricane?).

"So vhy ve came to vunderful U.S. from all contries? Crossink lend an' cease, in trains an' sheeps—"

"*Mr.* Kap—"

"—going t'rough tarrible hodsheeps to see et lest dat beauriful Statue Liberty? Ve came for vun plain rizzon: Becawss here ve got Friddom! Here ve are brodders! Here ve are 'Vun nation, inwisible, mit liberty an' Jostice free for all'!"

Mr. Parkhill wished he could lie down. But bright was the light in Molly Yanoff's eyes, deep the glow on Mr. Nussbaum's cheek. Even Oscar Trabish had traded somnolence for admiration.

"So look on vhat heppened in dis vary room a few minutes behind me! Who vas stendink here? A fine man. A good man. An immigrant de same as you an' me. Mr. P. I. Studniczka." (Mr. Studniczka looked up, thunderstruck.) "An' ven dat svitt saul makes his *foist spitch* to de cless, his foist chence to give a semple his English ve should all halp him ot, vhat he got? Sympaty? No! Unnistándink? No! Jostice? Phooey! He got fromm *soitin* fallow students"— Mr. Kaplan froze the blood of those unnamed—"shop voids, high-tone criticizink. Batter *ashame* should soitin pipple be!" Several of them, indeed, were already writhing in mortification.

Suddenly, Mr. Kaplan smiled at Reuben Olansky and, honey on his tongue, inquired: "Podden me, Olansky. How lonk you are in U.S.?"

Mr. Olansky blinked, as confused by the question as by his failure to locate its source.

"Mine dear Olansky, it's only a qvastion," purred Mr. Kaplan. "Are you tong-tie? How lonk you are in U.S.?"

"Seven years!" shouted Mr. Olansky. "I came—"

Mr. Kaplan raised a barricading palm. "Saven yiss. . . . My! *Saven* yiss! Not t'ree, not fife, but saven yiss!" Then he struck. "An' only in beginnis' grate!"

"Hanh?!" Mr. Olansky clawed at his forehead, livid, sputtering such mordant rejoinders in his native tongue that Mr. Parkhill began to hurry from the back row to the front.

"Studniczka, howlonkare *you* in U.S.?" called Mr. Kaplan.

All heads turned to Peter Studniczka; all ears pricked up; but Mr. Studniczka turned as maroon and speechless as a beet.

"Studniczka," Mr. Kaplan whispered, "you got to halp me ot. Like I'm your lawyer! Tell, Studniczka. De troot is de troot!" The clarion voice ascended. *"How lonk you in Amarica?"*

"Two year," strangled Mr. Studniczka.

Mr. Kaplan's whoop was pure rapture. "Only two yiss? *An' also in beginnis' cless!* You hoid, cless?! You hoid, Olansky?"

Mr. Olansky had not only heard, he had wheeled around in his chair, presenting his back in visible insult to Torquemada, and began hurling his chagrin at the rear window: "Should be a law against Koplan! . . . A coise on his liver. . . . The man is *meshuggeh.* . . ."

"Class—"

"Two yiss voisus *saven* yiss!" the stern advocate reminded the jury. "A mountain naxt to a moose! A new immigrant besite a man should alraddy hev his citizen papiss! . . . Olansky, hang your hat in shame! Studniczka, lift op your ice an' be prod! You—"

"Stop!" roared Mr. Olansky. "How long *are you in America*?"

"I'm comparink!" thundered Mr. Kaplan.

The bell pealed an end to the bloodletting. But the class milled around, arguing, inveighing, accusing, defending, praising Mr. Kaplan for his compassion or denouncing him for his prosecution, inflating Mr. Studniczka's prospects for progress or consoling apoplectic Olansky for his immolation. The brouhaha raged even as they collected their books and donned their coats, to file out at last, trailing farewells to their pastor.

"Good night . . ." Mr. Parkhill responded. "Good night . . ." He wanted a word with Mr. Kaplan, alone. He wanted to insist upon self-discipline, restraint, the renunciation of any more cunning wiles or crafty entrapments.

But Kaplan was halfway out of the door; and to his side hurried Mr. Studniczka, calling, "Mister! . . . Mister! . . ."

Mr. Kaplan turned.

"Mister." Mr. Studniczka fumbled with his mackinaw. "You talk good."

"Me?" Mr. Kaplan sighed. He gazed at his client. "You know how lonk *I'm* in Amarica?"

Mr. Studniczka shook his head.

"Fiftin yiss."

Mr. Studniczka blinked. "You—talk good."

Mr. Parkhill turned off the lights.

6

MR. PARKHILL'S BIRTHDAY

It was a miserable evening. All day long the rain had swept down in driving shafts, the way it used to pour on Camp Quinnipaquig, the summer he had spent there as a counsellor. Quinnipaquig. . . . That had been a pleasant summer, the lake blue-cold and ever-so-bracing. Mr. Parkhill remembered the time he—

The ormolu clock on the mantel chimed. It chimed as sweetly as the night he had first put it there, after they had read his father's will. He looked up: 5:30. It was a good time for a sherry, a Mozart record— Mr. Parkhill bolted out of his easy chair. Good gracious! He had been so absorbed in Suetonius that he had lost all track of time. Why, he had to meet his class at 7:30. Perhaps he would not go to the restaurant, after all. He could scramble a few eggs—no, he had forgotten to buy eggs that morning. Not forgotten, really; he simply had hated to brave that rain; and he had enjoyed the long day at home, and the thought of this evening's special treat.

He did not even put his bathrobe on its hanger, dressing so rapidly, wrestling into his jacket, his Burberry, tugging on his rubbers, jamming on his hat, swinging the battered briefcase off its hook (thank goodness he had corrected the homework that morning!), spearing his umbrella. He locked the door and hurried down the stairs.

73

Mrs. Mulvaney, who lived down the hall, was coming up, a yard wide, groaning under two wet shopping bags. He had to squeeze against the wall, holding his umbrella and briefcase over his head, panting, "Good evening, Mrs. Mulvaney," as she panted, " 'Tain't a fit night out for beast or man—not that the good Lord made the one different than the other!"

He tripped down the stairs ("Different than" . . . not one person in a thousand said "different from") and opened the big umbrella. The rain hammered on the dome.

It was only two blocks to his favorite restaurant. He slipped slightly on a piece of lettuce in front of the G. and R. grocery. (Someone really should report the G. and R. to the city; why, the sidewalk in front of their premises was halved by their discarded crates and cartons.)

Through the wet, fogged windows of La Belle Époque, the old-fashioned chandeliers beckoned.

"Some night, huh?" The doorman clucked.

"It certainly is."

Pierre opened the door for him, and Adolphe helped him take off his coat.

"I'm terribly late tonight," said Mr. Parkhill.

Adolphe looked astounded. "But eet is not yet even seex on clock, *m'sieur!*"

"I mean I have to be out by seven . . . my class. . . ."

"Ah, *dommage*. . . ." He led Mr. Parkhill to a table. There was no other patron in La Belle Époque so early.

He ordered quickly. And as he sipped his *apéritif,* he reached into his pocket and removed the lacy birthday card from Aunt Agatha, mailed, as it was every year, so as to arrive exactly on date, and containing, as it did each year, a crisp five-dollar bill with the tart instruction: "To be spent on something *foolish.*" Aunt Agatha always underlined the "foolish."

The other letter he had received (and what a pleasant

surprise that had been) was from Mr. Linton. He read it again:

The Tilsbury Academy
(founded 1802)
Old Tilsbury
Vermont

Office of the Headmaster

May 4

Dear Parkhill:

The other night, Mrs. Linton and I were reminiscing about past boys, and as we browsed through old school annuals together, we came upon your photograph (the year you were awarded the Ernestine Hopp Medal for School Spirit). Mrs. Linton reminded me of the time you astonished us all, as a freshman, by parsing that sentence from Cicero during tea. We laughed merrily.

The only other boy Mrs. Linton remembered so well was Wesley Collender ('38), who placed a copper contrivance in the fuse box at Farwell which expanded and contracted so that the "lights out" bell rang on and off, on and off, for a goodly ten minutes before Mr. Thistlewaite could ascertain the cause and effect the remedy! Thistlewaite is no longer with us. He is, I believe, at Claremont or Carmel or some such place in the western states that begins with "C."

Be that as it may, Mrs. Linton called my attention to the birthdate under your picture. "Why, that is next Tuesday!" she exclaimed, and indeed it was.

I extend, accordingly, our combined felicitations, and express our wishes for, in *loquendi usus,* "many happy returns!"

Faithfully yours,
Amos Royce Linton

P.S. What *are* you up to these days?

It had been awfully nice of Mr. Linton to write. The last time he had seen "Old Molasses," which was what the boys privately called Mr. Linton, was six years ago, when his class had presented the school with a carved newel-post for Modley Hall.

The clams were exceptionally sweet, he thought, this season. And the onion soup was delicious. No one made better onion soup than his mother had. When did he last —yes, the spring before she passed away, wraithlike and uncomplaining. Mr. Parkhill had just turned thirty. Her last words to him had been, "Be a good boy."

As he savored the kidneys *à la Grecque*, Mr. Parkhill remembered the first time he had gone back to visit Tilsbury. It was the year after he had received his B.A. He had worked so hard at Amherst that he had not had a real chance to visit the old school. He felt guilty about that.

When Mr. Linton had asked him what he was doing now, Mr. Parkhill told him he had taken a temporary post, as a substitute "just for the teaching experience," at the American Night Preparatory School for Adults.

"Parkhill," Mr. Linton had asked in his no-nonsense manner, "what on *earth* is that?"

"It is a night school, sir."

"College entrances? Cram courses? That sort of institution?"

"Oh, no, sir. This is an elementary school."

"A *what*? Speak up, Parkhill!"

"An *elementary* school, sir," Mr. Parkhill repeated. "For adults."

Mr. Linton must have gotten very hard of hearing, for he had gazed at Mr. Parkhill stonily and mumbled something that sounded like "Good God!" But that could not have been it; that was not at all like Mr. Linton; it was probably "Great Scott!"

Mr. Parkhill often found himself thinking back to that visit to Tilsbury. He could understand that a man like Mr. Linton had no way of knowing what a fine institution the

American Night Preparatory School for Adults really was. After all, Mr. Linton had led a rather sheltered life: Exeter, Harvard, Oxford. . . . (He wondered what Mr. Linton would have said when Hyman Kaplan named our leading institutions of higher learning as "Yale, Princeton and Hartford.") Mr. Linton always taught the senior Latin course— and what a strict drillmaster he had been! He would utter the most scathing remarks about a *lapsus linguae,* and even more acid ones about a *lapsus calami.*

Tilsbury. . . . What a different world that had been. Mr. Parkhill felt a rush of pleasant memories: that lovely campus, so tidy, green, serene, composed; the broad river that overflowed its banks in the spring; the school pond on bright winter days, a burnished mirror; the path across Main Quad that none but lordly seniors were permitted to use. . . . Those were happy days in a happy world, a world ten thousand miles and years away.

Occasionally, Mr. Parkhill caught himself wondering what it would have been like if he had returned to Tilsbury as a master. (In truth, Mr. Linton had never even sounded him out on that.) Life was curious. Who would have dreamed that Mr. Brockway, the teacher for whom Mr. Parkhill had been summoned to fill in "just for one or two sessions" at the American Night Preparatory School for Adults, would never return? Why, Mr. Robinson, the principal, could never even learn what had happened to him. Mr. Robinson was livid about such an unprofessional flight from duty, and had written several scathing letters to the New York Teachers Association, but the N.Y.T.A. had not been able to help Mr. Robinson very much; the only information they could relay was that Mr. Brockway had sent them a postcard from Acapulco, saying that two months at the American Night Preparatory School for Adults had driven him to the edge of a nervous breakdown, and should he regain his health he would rather take a job in a slaughterhouse than return to the A.N.P.S.A.

"Café, m'sieur?"

"Sanka, thank you."

Mr. Parkhill recalled how Aunt Agatha used to ask him, whenever he visited her, if he intended to spend the rest of his life among "those people in New York." Aunt Agatha, who had never even set foot in New York, did not understand the special rewards adult students provide someone who regards teaching not as a job, but as a mission. He had once had a little fun at Aunt Agatha's expense, saying, "Why, Aunt Agatha, just as grandfather Hewitt brought God to the heathen, I bring Grammar to the alien."

Aunt Agatha never brought up the subject again.

He glanced at his watch. How nice. There was time for a second cup of Sanka.

"Foreigners?" Mr. Linton had wheezed. "You teach *foreigners?*"

Mr. Parkhill wiped his mouth. He recalled the night Mr. Kaplan, cornered by his enemies, who demanded he explain the meaning of the "R.S.V.P" he had, in a reckless burst of elegance, tacked onto a letter composition, rejoined, "It minns 'Reply, vill you plizz?'" Even the memory made Mr. Parkhill smile.

He paid his bill, put on his coat and his rubbers, stepped into the street. The rain was not letting up.

He began to walk briskly, leaning into the deluge. He could hardly wait to get to the school. Sometimes, when he entered that old, unprepossessing building, he felt as if, like Alice, he was walking through a looking-glass into an antic and unpredictable land.

"Miss Goldberg . . . Mr. Fledermann . . ."

Mr. Parkhill could not help noticing that Mr. Kaplan had not yet arrived. The seat in the center of the front row, that seat directly in front of Mr. Parkhill's desk, was empty. When Mr. Kaplan occupied that place, he seemed to increase in size, until he blotted out the rest of the class; and when Mr. Kaplan was not in that seat, as now, it seemed as barren as Bald Mountain.

"Mrs. Pilpul . . . Mr. Wilkomirski . . . Miss Atrakian . . ."

It was not simply that the corporeal Mr. Kaplan was missing; the Big Dipper had disappeared.

"Miss Gidwitz . . ."

"Here."

"Mr. Nathan . . ."

"Ready for the show!" chuckled Nathan P. Nathan, sending Mr. Parkhill a disconcerting wink.

"Mr. Olansky . . ."

Mr. Olansky was nowhere to be seen. Mr. Parkhill worried about a man so near-sighted on a night such as this.

"Mr. Kap—"

Sam Pinsky cut the fateful name in half. "Mr. Keplen asked me I should say he is onawoidably ditained. But he will positively come!"

"Thank you." Mr. Parkhill put the attendance sheet to one side. "Well, class, suppose we complete our last meeting's—er—uncompleted Recitation and Speech."

"I have goose-dimples!" wailed Mrs. Moskowitz.

"From practice you will *learn*," chirped Miss Mitnick.

"I should live so long."

"Now, now, Mrs. Moskowitz," Mr. Parkhill smiled. "Nothing ventured, nothing gained." (And probably because of that letter from Mr. Linton, *Empta dolore docet experientia"* leaped into his mind. How appropriate: "Experience wrought with pain teaches.") The hand of Oscar Trabish rose limply.

"Yes?"

"What does that mean?"

"I beg your pardon?"

"What does it *mean?*" Mr. Trabish repeated. "Those words you just gave. About adwentures and games—"

"Ah!" Mr. Parkhill exclaimed. "I said 'Nothing ventured' —not 'adventured,' Mr. Trabish—'nothing gained,' not—er —'games.' That is a saying. It means that if we never try, how can we hope to succeed?"

"Psssh!" Mr. Pinsky goggled. "Will Mr. Keplen be mat he wasn't here to hear that!"

" 'Mad,' Mr. Pinsky, not 'mat.' And it really would be better to say that Mr. Kaplan will be 'disappointed' or 'sorry' instead of 'mad.' After all, 'mad' means insane—er —crazy."

"Exoct worrd for thot mon!" declared Miss Tarnova.

"Wait till Mr. Keplen comes before you insult!" snapped indignant Pinsky.

Mr. Barbella gave a derisive laugh. "Ifa Kaplan scratches, Pinsky hollers 'Ouch!' Ifa you tickle Kaplan, Pinsky makes 'Ha, ha!' "

Mr. Pinsky turned on Lucca Barbella, trying to bestow upon him that glare, compounded of ice and fire, with which Mr. Kaplan froze the blood of his foes.

"You look like Cholly Chaplin, not Hymie Kaplen!" mocked Mr. Nussbaum, fingering an earlock.

"That's *right!*" laughed Mr. Nathan. "Pinsky practice—"

"Mrs. Pilpul," Mr. Parkhill called quickly. "Your recitation."

A cantata of encouragement launched the widow Pilpul on her fearful path. She moved her chair, smoothed her hair, soothed her morale, and proved her mettle by answering a question no one had asked: "So what's to be afraid?"

"Sure!"

"Soitinly!"

"So what's the worst can heppen?" asked "Cookie" Kipnis.

"The woist can happen is I'll make a million mistakes," said Minnie Pilpul.

This fusion of courage and stoicism garnered new praises from the gallery.

"Good fa you, Mrs.!"

"That's a spirit!"

"Best weeshes!" sang Lola Lopez.

Mrs. Pilpul, having marched to the front with stately tread, placed one hand on the desk (it looked for a moment as if she were reeling, but she was only twisting or stretching), placed the other hand on her hip and caroled:

"Roses are ret
Wiolets are blue
Sugar is sveet
And so are you!

"This kindergarten pome I just said," Mrs. Pilpul announced, "is learned by all the kitties in America. Just like my little goil, Hinda, age hate, from who I learned it. So why I am taking time in Racitation and Speech to say this simple nurse's rhyme?"

"Why?" asked Mr. Vinograd, who favored the literal.

"Because the woild would be a better place all around *if grown-ops behaved more like kitties!* Honist and nice! If Congriss was more like kindergarten, would maybe be less graft, crime and wiolence! . . . Everybody: Remember children!" With that exhortation, Mrs. Pilpul stalked back to her place.

She barely had time to regain it before hands were bobbing up and down like buoys in a squall. The most energetic bobbing was effected by Mr. Olansky, who had entered the room some time ago.

Mr. Parkhill called on Mr. Blattberg, who opened the postmortem by observing that Mrs. Pilpul had used "goil" instead of "girl" and "woild" instead of "world." (Mr. Blattberg had come a long way since his initiation into the beginners' grade.)

Miss Gidwitz remarked that Mrs. Pilpul "used 'hate,' which is for hating, instead of 'eight' which is for telling age!"

Stanislaus Wilkomirski deplored the fact that Mrs. Pilpul kept saying "kitties" when she obviously meant "more than one children."

Mr. Barbella electrified the academicians by challenging Mrs. Pilpul's naïve panacea: anyone familiar with either children *or* kindergartens, Mr. Barbella hotly observed, knew that our little ones would "chop off da heads" of all within reach if but possessed of the weapons and provided with the opportunity.

"Shame! Skaptic! Cynic!" hissed Olga Tarnova.

Mr. Barbella cried, "Name of the name!" in Italian.

Miss Tarnova volleyed a scorching rejoinder in Russian. *"Vryét—"*

"Class, please!" Mr. Parkhill intervened. "Let us limit our discussion to Mrs. Pilpul's *English.* There were several mistakes in pronunciation—which have not yet been mentioned. They occurred in Mrs. Pilpul's first two sentences!"

The class dived deep into memory to retrieve Mrs. Pilpul's first two sentences. Their diving produced symptoms of asphyxiation.

"The rhyme began," hinted Mr. Parkhill, " 'Roses are red . . .' "

The class reconstructed "Roses are red" without a single spotting of Mrs. Pilpul's "ret".

"The next line was 'Violets are blue . . .' "

No one seemed to have noticed how the widow Pilpul had mispronounced "violets."

Mr. Parkhill turned to the board and printed:

RED   VIOLETS
RET   WIOLETS

82

"The two top words tell us exactly how they should be pronounced. But Mrs. Pilpul pronounced them as I have written them, incorrectly, in the lower words."

To his surprise, not a single "Oh," "Ah," or "Hoo Ha!" ascended (although Mr. Nathan winked again).

"Let me show you how important that is. For example . . ." On the board Mr. Parkhill printed:

PEAS
PEACE

"Now, class, there is all the difference in the world between 'pea*z*,' which we eat, and 'pea*ss*,' which we—long for."

Now the "Ah!"'s and "Ooh!"'s ascended, crowned by a reverent "Holy smoky!" from Isaac Nussbaum.

"Now, class, concentrate on this. . . ." He stepped to the next board, on which he limned:

1. CLOSE
2. CLOSE

addressing his flock over his shoulder: "If we pronounce 'close' with an 's'—thus, 'clos*sse*'—it is an adjective, meaning 'near' or—er—'stuffy.' 'Come close to me,' or 'It is a bit close in the room tonight.' . . . But if we pronounce these *very same letters* as 'close,' with a 'z,' the word becomes a verb, with a *wholly* different meaning: 'to shut,' as in 'Please close the window,' or 'Do close the door'—"

In uncanny dramatization (albeit in reverse) the door was flung open. A gust of cold dampness swept across the scholars. All heads swung to the doorway as one—there to behold, his face wet, his smile incandescent, his hair wreathed in a halo of mist—

"Mr. Kaplan!" cried Fanny Gidwitz.

"Et lest!" grinned Sam Pinsky.

"Mm-mnh," yawned Oscar Trabish.

Not all his peers greeted Mr. Kaplan in such joyous accents.

"About time!" scowled Mr. Olansky, consulting his watch to see what time it actually was.

"Did you had to stop on the way at City Hall?" sneered Mrs. Yanoff.

"Ara you coming or going?" inquired Vasil Hruska, the "coming" swathed in regret, the "going" fraught with desire.

The hostile sentiments roused Mr. Pinsky to a retort of pure inspiration: "Mr. Keplen isn't late; the class is *early!*"

Mr. Nathan flung his head back, transported. "Kapalan's brain is like the flu—it's spreading!"

"Good evening, Mr. Kaplan," said Mr. Parkhill.

It was just like Mr. Kaplan to enter the room that way. Any other student arriving this late would have courted invisibility, as Mr. Olansky had, opening the door like a mouse, tiptoeing in like a thief, creeping to the nearest vacant haven. Not Hyman Kaplan. He could not even arrive late without endowing it with the flourishes of a world premiere. From the smile he was now dispensing to the rabble who had taunted him, one would think his tardiness called for public celebration.

"Come in . . ." Mr. Parkhill noticed that Mr. Pinsky was signaling to Mr. Kaplan with surreptitious flippings of his hand and *sotto voce* "Psst! Psst!"'s. Mr. Kaplan nodded but made not the slightest move into the room.

"Do join us," said Mr. Parkhill dryly.

"Axcuse me," said Mr. Kaplan. "You are blocking de dask."

Mr. Parkhill could hardly have been more astonished. He had indeed moved from the blackboard to the side of the desk nearest the door; but why that should impede Mr. Kaplan's passage from the door to his seat, a path entirely unobstructed by Mr. Parkhill *or* the desk. . . . "Mr. Kaplan," Mr. Parkhill replied frostily, "you may take your seat—"

He never finished, for the moment he started to turn back to the board (where he wanted to add "Night . . . knight" as yet another example of the prickly pairing of sounds/spelling) Mr. Kaplan lunged toward the desk, whipped a large object from behind his back, plopped it on the desk, and cried, "Soprise!"

The class, which had remained unusually quiet (now that Mr. Parkhill thought of it), erupted.

"Congrajulation!"

"Happy boitday!"

"A hondritt more!"

The Messrs. Wodjik croaked in unison, "Present is from *all!*"

Mr. Parkhill flushed. So that was why Mr. Kaplan was so late . . . and why he had made so odd an entrance . . . and why he had offered no apology for so tardy an arrival. He had been shopping. . . . But how in the world had they found out it was his birthday?

Mr. Kaplan was pointing to the parcel rather like one of the prophets on the Sistine ceiling. "Plizz open op. It's a prazant."

"Let all have a look," called Lola Lopez.

"Maybe Mr. Parkhill already hos it?" Miss Tarnova intoned in typical premonitory gloom.

"Impossible!" Mr. Kaplan glowered.

"*Noh*thing is impossible," moaned the fatalist.

"Look in a mirror," purred Mr. Kaplan.

"Shah!" called Mrs. Moskowitz.

"Ze class muzt be *quiet* quiet!" commanded C. J. Fledermann.

The sounds fled into the tunnel of silence.

Mr. Parkhill glanced around. "I—uh—I hardly know what to say."

"*You* don't know what say?" echoed Mr. Studniczka in astonishment.

"Don't say. Enjoy!" called Minnie Pilpul.

Mr. Kaplan raised an imperial hand. "Attention, class. Mr. Pockheel . . ."

Mr. Parkhill tugged at the wrapping. The paper was gold, but the band of ribbon was white, tied in a bow the size of a cantaloupe, and wet, which made it very hard to rip or split or even stretch.

"Tear it!"

"*Pull,* maybe."

"Cot with a knife.!"

"From the site!"

He managed to separate the cantaloupe and the ribbon and peeled off the gold-colored paper. As the last damp strip of paper dropped away, he opened the box. There lay an attaché case.

"Take ot and hold op," whispered Mr. Kaplan.

Mr. Parkhill executed the instructions.

"Psssh!" cried Mr. Pinsky, slapping his cheek in ecstasy. "Is dat *beautiful!*"

"*Bella, bella!*" That, of course, was Lucca Barbella.

"Use in best of halth!" called the widow Pilpul.

Mr. Kaplan passed his lighthouse beam across the ranks, inquiring *sotto voce,* "How's abot mine choice?"

"Fine!"

"I gotta admit!"

"Poifict!"

Mr. Kaplan accepted their accolade.

Mr. Parkhill wiped his palms. "Class, this is—*very* kind of you—"

"Mr. Pockheel!" Mr. Kaplan's pain was unmistakable. "Your acknowledgink comms *efter* my prezantink!"

"I beg your pardon."

Mr. Kaplan faced his confrères, raised his arms, inclined his head in the gracious manner of the Prince Royal distributing prizes at a rustic bazaar, and orated: "Distingvished titcher in American Prep School for Adolts—" (Mr. Parkhill wondered why it had never occurred to him to call the A.N.P.S.A. a prep school.) "—tonight ve have a fine occasion. Soch an occasion comms only vunce a year to eny man, only vunce a year iven to our titcher!" Mr. Kaplan paused for the applause he deemed appropriate; it came; it departed at a wiggle of Mr. Kaplan's forefinger. "So tonight ve salebrate Mr. Pockheel's boitday. Ve have no fency *program,* ufcawss. Still an' all—"

"Make short, in Gott's name!" implored Mr. Olansky.

"The Constitution didn't take so long!" laughed Mr. Nathan. "Rose Mitnick is supposed to make the speech!"

"Call Miss Mitnick!"

"Miss Mitnick!" "Rose Mitnick!" came a dozen rebellious cries.

"You'll *gat* Mitnick." Mr. Kaplan's *noblesse oblige* indicated that there is no accounting for human folly. "So, now, fallow students, to *prezant* de prazent givink our rizzons for how ve chose it, an' a full dascription of de insite, ve vill hear from de *odder* member of de Boitday Prazent Committee! Hau Kay, take de floor, Mitnick."

But Miss Mitnick had slumped so deep in her chair she was neither visible nor audible.

"Mitnick . . ." murmured Mr. Kaplan.

The wan maiden's skin had turned the color of a squirrel.

"Talk!" begged Mr. Kaplan.

But Miss Mitnick could not talk: her lips were parted but her tongue was paralyzed.

*"Mit*nick!" called Mr. Kaplan urgently.

Miss Mitnick had turned to stone.

"She has stage-fried!" cried Fanny Gidwitz.

"Swallowed her tong!" mourned "Cookie" Kipnis.

"She's just nervous," laughed Nathan P. Nathan. "Rosie, make your speech!"

Even the voice of her courter fell deaf on Rose Mitnick's ears.

"Mitnick, Miss Mitnick, stand *op,* Rose Mitnick!"

moaned Mrs. Moskowitz. It had the cadence of a dirge.

Petrified, her hair as distraught as her larynx, Miss Mitnick lay supine, a limp chrysanthemum.

"Sombody slep her hends!" cried Mr. Kaplan.

"Make on her 'Boo'!"

"Snep fingers!"

"Could be her shoes are too tight," ventured Mr. Pinsky, with professional expertise. "She nids at least a 5-B."

The contralto of Olga Tarnova ululated above the others. "Wonce I saw octress had seemilar choke-in-troat. Eight minutes. In Rossia. In weenter. By lohver's ronning away with soprano. Oh, was sod, sod." (Miss Tarnova could not utter "Hello" without conjuring up some tragic image from the frozen steppes.)

Mr. Kaplan was staring at Miss Mitnick with as much horror as she was gaping at him in terror. "Mitnick," he pleaded, "it's not for *me*. Remamber! It's for Mr. *Pockheel!*"

No other tocsin could have penetrated Miss Mitnick's benumbment. She struggled to her feet, a convulsive automaton, her glazed eyes aimed at the middle of Mr. Parkhill's chest; panting, by a heroic act of will, she staggered forward and into the fire: "On behalf of beginners' grade and all the students in it, I present this little key—" Miss Mitnick stopped. "—key—" she gibbered. "Key . . . *key*?!"

"Give her the *key!*" laughed Mr. Nathan.

Mr. Kaplan snapped his fingers in apology, and pulled a red ribbon from his pocket, a ribbon from which two tiny keys sparkled. *"Two* keys," he whispered. "Make plural."

Miss Mitnick took the ribbon and held it forth stiffly. "I present these keys, to now open the guaranteed genuine leather, full-lined, solid-brass-hinges case for Mr. Parkhill!"

Now it was done. Hurrahs. Applause. A fanfare of felicitations. A hush.

They were all beaming at Mr. Parkhill.

He coughed. "Thank you. What a thoughtful—surprise! I—am most grateful. It's very kind of you, all of you. Thank you ever so much."

"Aupen op de case!"

As Mr. Parkhill fitted one of the little keys into the lock, he noticed that the case was initialed: "M. P." . . . "M. P."? How strange: "M. P." stood for "Mounted Police" or "Member of Parliament." His initials were not "M. P." His first name did not even begin with "M."

The rain was slashing at the windows, and the distant city noises signaled their intimations of the raffish. At Tilsbury, the peepers heralded each spring in night whistlings so constant and melodious that none who first heard them could believe his ears. Some visitors simply could not believe that the peepers were frogs, not bobolinks. . . . Suddenly, Mr. Parkhill recalled the odd expression on Mr. Linton's face that time he had told him about the American Night Preparatory School for Adults. Then Aunt Agatha's prim features swam into recollection. . . .

Mr. Parkhill looked up. The faces that loomed before him were larger than life, it seemed: Mr. Kaplan, Miss Mitnick, Miss Tarnova . . . Pinsky, Olansky, Gidwitz . . . They seemed united, for once, in unfamiliar concord.

And revelation explained the initials on the case. "M. P." Obviously. The class always called him "Mr. Parkhill." The occasion had never arisen for them to know, or for him to tell, his first name.

Why, he could hardly remember the last time anyone had addressed him by it.

7

MR. K·A·P·L·A·N AND
THE INEXCUSABLE "FEH!"

"Fata viam invenient," Mr. Parkhill reflected, as he called
the beginners' grade to order. "Fate will find a way." Vergil
—that was who had said it. It was a consoling maxim; and
Mr. Parkhill clung to it as he called the roll.

"Mr. Vinograd."

"Here."

"Lola Lopez."

"Si!"

"Mr. Peter Studniczka."

"Yo."

"Mr. Kaplan."

No answer.

"Mr. Kaplan?" repeated Mr. Parkhill, aiming his glance
directly at Hyman Kaplan, who reclined in his established
site in the very kernel of the front row.

Still no answer.

Mr. Parkhill frowned. "Mr. *Kap*lan!" he called for the
third time, quite firmly, forcing Mr. Kaplan's gaze to meet
his own. Forcing? No; Mr. Kaplan's eyes had been waiting
for a rendezvous with Mr. Parkhill's all the time. It was
only when he was certain that Mr. Parkhill was observing
his every movement that Mr. Kaplan narrowed his eyes
and turned to throw a withering glare at the occupant of
the chair at the left end of the front row. In a tone dripping

disdain, the thrice-named scholar intoned, "Keplen is in place."

Mr. Parkhill adjusted his glasses uneasily. "Mrs. Pilpul . . ."

Mr. Parkhill did not like the look of things; he did not like the look of things at all. When Hyman Kaplan flung the gauntlet down at the opening of an evening, in so slow and sententious a manner, a fracas surely lay in the offing. And from the buzzings and "Pss! Pss!"ings that bounced from one camp to another in the room, Mr. Parkhill sensed that the class, too, had read the ominous meaning in Mr. Kaplan's pantomime. That slitting of the eyes, that lethal stare, that doomsday tone—to anyone who knew Hyman Kaplan these signified but one thing: Hyman Kaplan had issued that deadly warning which precedes a declaration of war. There could be no doubt about it.

"But why?" Mr. Parkhill wondered. Whenever Mr. Kaplan bestowed so scorching a glare on a colleague, it was for one reason: his honor had been slurred, and demanded satisfaction.

Who was the villain at the left end of the front row? He was one Fischel Pfeiffer. He had registered in Miss Higby's class; but Miss Higby had just marched Mr. Pfeiffer into Mr. Parkhill's room, handed Mr. Parkhill a slip of paper, and whispered that, although Fischel Pfeiffer was a rare and dedicated pupil, a student of undeniable promise, he was "not quite ready" for the heady heights of Advanced Grammar and Civics.

"Why not?" Mr. Parkhill had whispered back.

"You'll see," Miss Higby rewhispered, with a cunning smile. (Mr. Parkhill wished that Miss Higby, who could be so forthright about things like "Drill, drill, drill!," would not suddenly wallow in innuendo.)

During the two teachers' muted exchange, Mr. Pfeiffer had remained standing, silent, baleful, lips tight, his expression a testament to despond. None but the blind could have misread his mood: Mr. Pfeiffer was mortified by demotion.

He was a dapper man with a foppish mustache, a polka-dot tie, a cream-colored suit the sleeves of which stood out as sharply as two razors.

"Good luck," Miss Higby murmured, tripping out of the room.

Mr. Parkhill turned to greet his new charge. "We're glad to have you with us." He offered a reassuring smile. (At least it reassured Mr. Parkhill; it made no dent on Mr. Pfeiffer.)

"Class, this is"—he glanced at the name on the transfer slip—"Mr. Pfeiffer, Mr.—er—Fischel Pfeiffer. . . . Won't you take a seat, please?"

From the miasma of his discontent, Fischel Pfeiffer surveyed the Siberia to which he had been exiled.

"There is a place right there—in the front row," suggested Mr. Parkhill lightly.

Without a word, Mr. Pfeiffer limped toward the empty chair at the left end of the front row. It was at that moment that Mr. Parkhill had felt a premonitory twinge: in order to reach the seat at the end of the front row, Mr. Pfeiffer was obliged to pass directly in front of Mr. Kaplan. And Mr. Kaplan, leaning far forward, presumably to retrieve a pencil which had not dropped to the floor, had followed every word of the dialogue between Miss Higby and Mr. Parkhill with the keenest fascination. . . .

As Mr. Pfeiffer crossed in front of Mr. Kaplan, that self-appointed protector of the homeless had sung out, "Valcome, Fischel Pfeiffer! Valcome to beginnis' grate!"

The new pupil had paused, appraised his unsolicited cicerone with glacial disesteem, and uttered a monosyllable the mere recollection of which made Mr. Parkhill's forehead dampen: "Feh!"

That was all Fischel Pfeiffer had said: "Feh!"

Now "Feh!" was an expletive Mr. Parkhill had heard before—but in the *corridors* of the American Night Preparatory School for Adults, never inside his classroom. The expression had, in fact, intrigued him as a fine example of onomatopoeia. Just as "moo" or "quack" or "coo" convey their meaning with faultless accuracy, so "Feh!" is a vivid, if inelegant, vehicle for the communication of distaste.

"Feh!" The class had caught its collective breath, then turned from Fischel Pfeiffer to Hyman Kaplan, a man renowned for sensitivity.

His jaw had dropped: "Feh?" Mr. Kaplan echoed dazedly. "Feh for de *cless?!*"

"Our exercise tonight is Open Questions," Mr. Parkhill quickly announced. Long experience had taught him to recognize the first alarums of discord, and how to canalize hostility by diverting attention. "The floor is open, class. Any questions at all. Any problems in English you may have encountered in reading, or writing, conversation. . . . Who will begin?"

Up rose the irate hand of Sam Pinsky.

"Mr. Pinsky?"

"I ebsolutely agree with Mr. Keplen!" proclaimed Mr. Pinsky. "A member shouldn't make 'Feh!' for the class!"

"That," said Mr. Parkhill crossly, "is not a question."

The unsure finger of Lola Lopez signaled for enlightenment.

"Miss Lopez?"

"Why 'sceessors' has a 'c' and 's' but not 'z's?" asked Lola Lopez. "I *hear* 'z's!" (The spelling of that dreadful word "scissors," Mr. Parkhill brooded, must have plagued every student and teacher in every English course in the land.)

"I'm afraid 'scissors' just is spelled that way," Mr. Parkhill replied with regret. "As we have often seen, many

93

words in English unfortunately do not look at *all* the way they—er—sound."

" 'Fight'!" laughed Nathan P. Nathan.

"Very good."

" 'Psychology'!" offered C. J. Fledermann.

"Excellent! . . . To get back to Open Questions . . ."

Lucca Barbella asked, with a certain bellicosity, "When doesa 'i' precedes 'e' and when 'e' precedes 'i'?"

"There is a useful little rhyme about that!" Mr. Parkhill smiled. "Don't you remember it, Mr. Barbella?"

"No."

Mr. Parkhill cleared his throat:

> "Put 'i' before 'e' except after 'c'
> Or when sounded as 'a'
> As in 'neighbor 'and' weigh'!

Remember?"

"I wasa absent."

"Sometimes you are ebsent vhen you are prazant," observed Hyman Kaplan.

Mr. Barbella damned him in Italian, which caused Nathan P. Nathan to acclaim him with laughter.

"Class . . . Miss Ziev?"

"Where is Denever?"

Deftly did Mr. Parkhill work his way through the next series of questions, a succession of sonar snares and orthographic delusions. Yet he could not shake off a sense of foreboding; for in the caverns below consciousness, the ominous, flatulent "Feh!" of Fischel Pfeiffer still reverberated.

It was hard enough to preserve decorum in a class torn by fierce vendettas, a class that included such antagonistic personalities as Hyman Kaplan and Reuben Olansky, or Mr. Kaplan and Aaron Blattberg, or Mr. Kaplan and Miss Mitnick. To add to this scholastic powderkeg a Fischel

Pfeiffer, a man foolhardy enough to affront Hyman Kaplan—Mr. Parkhill felt a surge of outright annoyance with Miss Higby.

When Open Questions ran dry, Mr. Parkhill announced, "Now, class, suppose we try a review drill on—vocabulary. Pencils and paper, please . . ."

The room rustled like aspens in the wind.

"I shall write five words on the blackboard. Simply use each word in a sentence, a—er—*full* sentence, that is. Five words, therefore five sentences," he smiled. "Compose your sentences carefully. Remember, I shall grade not just your spelling but your grammar, punctuation, use of *other* words. . . ."

Mrs. Moskowitz began to fan herself with her notebook. It was hard enough for Mrs. Moskowitz to spell one word right; to spell five correctly, and employ them in sentences in which all the other words had to be spelled right, and selected properly, and fitted into the stubborn architecture of syntax—that, for Mrs. Moskowitz, was virtually a sentence to Devil's Island.

Mr. Parkhill turned to the blackboard. In large block letters, he printed:

1. CHISEL
2. FIZZLE
3. GROAN
4. INCOME
5. CLIMAX

"Ooy!" came from unnerved Mrs. Moskowitz.

"Moskovitz," called Mr. Kaplan, "make santances, not funerals!"

Mr. Parkhill moved down the aisle. How pregnant the prelude to commitment always was. The class was scrutinizing the board as if it was a forest in which unseen snipers lurked in ambush. They reconnoitered "chisel" warily, flinched before "fizzle," hurdled guileless "groan" to reach forthright "income," pausing for second wind, so to speak, before taking the measure of the word which Mr. Parkhill, with playful accuracy, had chosen to complete the maze: "climax."

"I'm sure you all know the meaning of these words," said Mr. Parkhill.

"I," wheezed Olga Tarnova, "om not."

"Come, come, Miss Tarnova. Relax."

The sultry brunette heaved into the unknown.

Miss Mitnick had already bent her head over her notebook, the bun of her hair a doughnut on the nape of her demure neck. Beside her, Nathan P. Nathan was all admiration. Mr. Olansky had unbuttoned his vest, cleaned his bifocals, pressed his Scripto, shaken it from habit of years of struggle with fountain pens, and inscribed his first sentence. And Mr. Kaplan cocked his head to one side, repeated each word aloud in a clear, loud whisper, added an admiring "My!" or "Tchk!" of homage to Mr. Parkhill's gifts as a teacher, exclaimed, "Fife *fine* voids!" and shot Fischel Pfeiffer a glare designed to inform that churl of the riches which the beginners' grade spread before the worthy.

Mr. Fischel Pfeiffer never saw the reprimand. After one swift glance at the board, the mustached malcontent set to work with startling speed. Before most students had even cleared the troubling reefs of "chisel," Fischel Pfeiffer slapped his pencil down and announced, "Done!"

The appearance of a whirling dervish would have caused no greater astonishment.

"Done?"

"Finished?"

"So fest?"

Heads were popping up, mouths popping open, all around the congregation.

"We have here a *ginius?*" asked "Cookie" Kipnis.

"A regular spid demon?" Mr. Nussbaum queried.

"Pfeiffer expects to greduate before midnight!" rasped Mr. Pinsky, glancing toward his captain for approval. But Mr. Kaplan looked as if he had run into Beelzebub.

Before the sensation created by Mr. Pfeiffer's velocity had spent its force, that dapper gentleman had reached the blackboard, where he began to transcribe his sentences with an alacrity never before seen in the beginners' grade.

"We generally *wait* to go to the board until I—" Mr. Parkhill's voice trailed off.

Words were flowing from Mr. Pfeiffer's chalk as if from a magic wand.

All work amongst the watchers stopped. The class sat transfixed. Then a chorus of "Oh!"s and "Ah!"s and "Fentestic!"s rent the air. For on that plain, black board, in most beautiful script, Fischel Pfeiffer had written:

1. In Detroit Michigan she saw shiny Chinese bracelets in shops, ingraved by sharp *chisels*.

A hymn of admiration ascended from the seated—not only for the exquisite calligraphy, which would have done credit to a Persian, but for the mettle of a man brave enough to tackle names as prickly as "Detroit Michigan," or a phrase as exotic as "Chinese bracelets."

"Such panmanship!" marveled C. J. Fledermann.

"He writes like an artiss!" cried Minnie Pilpul.

"*Like* an arteest? No! He *is* an arteest!" throbbed Miss Tarnova. "This mon has soffert! This mon has soul!" (Olga Tarnova divided humanity into two unalterable groups: those with and those without "soul.")

Glee gushed from Mr. Blattberg. "Keplan, are you watching?"

"Pfeiffer makes you look like a greenhorn!" jeered Reuben Olansky, searching for the greenhorn through his bifocals.

Mr. Kaplan said nothing. He was pale, staring at the board where Mr. Pfeiffer was finishing his second sentence:

2. Soda waters are waters which they *fizzle.*

Now the "Oh!"s and the "Ah!"s burst like fireworks, topped by one reverential rocket: "Supoib!"

"Mamma mia!" gasped Lucca Barbella.

"Mr. Pfeiffer is raddy for college!" announced Mr. Vinograd.

"Now, now, class. Order. . . ." To tell the truth, Mr. Parkhill was as impressed as his charges. And why not? His years in the beginners' grade had taught him to expect for a sentence using "chisel," say, "I have a chisel," or "Give me chisels," or even "I like chisels." As for a word like "fizzle" . . .

Mr. Pfeiffer transferred three more sentences to the board with a rapidity and certitude that were to become a legend in the American Night Preparatory School for Adults:

3. Life is not only tears and *groans.*
4. Good *income* beats diamonds.
5. What is Man? Bird? Beest? No. God's *climax.*

To a symphony of praises as spirited as any Mr. Parkhill had ever heard in the classroom, Fischel Pfeiffer turned from the board, flecked a hair from a creamy sleeve, and returned to his seat.

"Boy!" laughed Mr. Nathan.

"Wohnderful," crooned Olga Tarnova. *"Khoroscho!"*

"Koplan," mocked Mr. Olansky, "you have nothing to say? Not one single criticize?"

Not only had Mr. Kaplan nothing to say, he seemed to

have no place to go. He was slumped so low in his chair that his shoulders were where his hips should have been.

"You look like a pencake!" crowed Mr. Blattberg.

Mr. Parkhill felt sorry for Hyman Kaplan. True, a man with so reckless a confidence and so luxuriant an ego might well expect to meet occasional reverses. Still, Mr. Kaplan had a certain proud flair, a daring, a *panache* not often found among the earthbound.

"Time is passing, class," said Mr. Parkhill. "Finish your assignment."

The class pulled unwilling eyes from the ornamented slate. They sighed and stirred and wrote their own humbled sentences. Soon Mr. Parkhill sent six students to the board. They copied their sentences dutifully, but the heart seemed to have gone out of them. For before all their eyes, like an unscalable summit, shone the glittering coinage of Fischel Pfeiffer.

How feeble, by comparison, seemed Mr. Hruska's "Actors give big *groans.*" How lackluster lay Miss Gidwitz's "The rain *fizzled.*" How jejune looked even C. J. Fledermann's foray into aesthetics: "Hungarian music has glorious *climax.*"

With apologetic phrases and self-deprecating shrugs, the listless six shuffled back to their places.

"Good!" said Mr. Parkhill brightly. "Discussion . . . Miss Ziev, will you read your sentences first?"

Miss Ziev, who had become more vivacious since Mr. Andrassy (in Mr. Krout's class) had repledged his troth, read her sentences, but dully—and the discussion thereof died stillborn. Not a scoff greeted even Miss Ziev's "The boy has certainly *groan* lately."

Peter Studniczka followed Miss Ziev, and not one outburst of "Mistake!" or "Hoo ha!" greeted Mr. Studniczka's "In bank are 2 doors: In come and Push Out."

Lola Lopez followed Mr. Studniczka, and Mr. Parkhill,

99

unable to inspirit his charges, had to carry the entire discussion by himself—even unto Miss Lopez's defiant, "Brazil has a nice, hot *climax.*"

The desultory response persisted even to Mr. Pinsky's alarming use of "chisel." (Mr. Pinsky seemed to consider "chisel" the diminutive of "cheese," hence his "Before sleep, I like a little milk and *chisel.*")

It was Mr. Parkhill alone who pointed out lapses in diction, the stumbling of syntax, the marooning of prepositions. The very heart of discussion had expired in the beginners' grade. Gone were the *sine quibus non* of debate: strong convictions, bravely held; the clash of opinions fiercely defended; the invaluable friction of a pupil certain he is right rubbing against another unaware she is wrong. . . .

Now only Mr. Pfeiffer's sentences remained to be read aloud. Mr. Parkhill teetered back and forth on his heels. "Mr. Pfeiffer, will you please read your work?"

A hush. All waited. All listened. And what all then heard, in indescribable astonishment (Mr. Pfeiffer had only opened his mouth twice, once for that unforgivable "Feh!" and then for that arrogant "Done!"), was a high, thin, squeaky sibilance: "In Detroit Missigan see saw siny Sinese braceletss in sops, ingraved by sarp tsiselss." There was no getting around it: Mr. Pfeiffer had said "Missigan" for "Michigan," "see saw" for "she saw," "siny" for "shiny," "sops" and "sarp"—

"A Litvak!" rang out a clarion voice. It was Mr. Kaplan. "Mein Gott, he's a *Litvak!*" He wheeled toward Mr. Parkhill. "Must be! From Lit'uania! He prononces a 'sh' like a hiss stimm—"

The heavens split above the beginners' grade.

"Shame, Koplon," howled Miss Tarnova.

"Can Pfeiffer *help* it he's a foreigner?" protested C. J. Fledermann.

"He's a foreigner *and* a Litvak," cried Hyman Kaplan.

100

"In class is no place to condemn!" shouted Mr. Olansky.

"To descripe," said Mr. Kaplan, "is not to condamn!"

The riposte only fanned the flames that swept through the battalion of Fischel Pfeiffer's admirers.

"Not fair!" charged Mr. Blattberg hotly.

"Not fair?" purred Mr. Kaplan. "If a student calls a shoe a 'soo' should ve give him a banqvet an' sing 'Hooray, hooray, he's ruinink English'?!"

"But discussion should be about the *work,*" sputtered Miss Atrakian, "not the *personal.*"

"Mine remocks are prononciational, not poisonal!" rejoined Mr. Kaplan.

Mr. Nathan was having a fit.

"Class, *class,*" Mr. Parkhill kept saying, "there's just no reason for such—"

"Keplan, you are *bad!*" blurted Isaac Nussbaum. (Mr. Nussbaum, who was pious, tended to confuse error with sin.) "Mr. Pfeiffer writes like a king!"

"Ha!" scoffed Mr. Kaplan. "He can write like a kink but he talks like a Litvak!"

*"Gent*lemen—"

"Kaplan, you jalous!" seethed Mr. Hruska.

"Who's makink poisonal remocks now?" leered Mr. Kaplan.

"Mr. Kap—"

"Stop!" boomed Reuben Olansky. "Mr. Hruska put his finger on! Koplan picks on tiny ditails!"

"A fishbone is tiny, but ken choke you to dat!"

"Mr. Pfeiffer's words are so fine, so what if he recites not perfect?" pleaded Miss Mitnick.

"A mistake," said Mr. Kaplan, "is a mistake."

"Mr. Pfeiffer needs praise, not pins!" railed the widow Pilpul.

"Are ve in cless to praise—or to loin?" flashed Mr. Kaplan.

"You don't give the Litvak a chence!" cried Mrs. Moskowitz.

"I vouldn't give an *Eskimo* a chence to wrack English!" Mr. Nathan was shaking like a man made of Jell-O.

"Kaplin, give an inch!" came Bessie Shimmelfarb's overdue plea for accommodation. "Just *vunce,* give an *inch!*"

Mr. Kaplan placed truth above measurement.

"You have to make allowance for frands!" stormed Mr. Blattberg.

"If mine own brodder made soch mistake," Mr. Kaplan retorted, "should I give him the Nobles Prize? If Pinsky makes a mistake, does Keplen say, 'Skip, skip, maybe he's a cousin Alfred Einstein's'?"

*"Gent*lemen!"

"What's Einstein got to do with Pfeiffer?" asked bewildered Milas Wodjik.

"What's Pfeiffer got to do with Einstein?" snapped Tomas Wodjik.

"Koplon, Koplon, whare is your *pity?"* beseeched Miss Tarnova.

"Piddy?" Mr. Kaplan shot up like a flagpole. "You esk piddy for *de man who sad 'Feh!' to de cless?!"*

And now Mr. Parkhill understood Mr. Kaplan's wrath, his outrage, his unyielding fusillade. "Class, there is no need for such heated dispute! Nothing is gained by passion," he said. "We are all—" The upraised thumb of Mr. Pinsky caught his eye. "Yes?"

"How do you spall 'passion'?"

Mr. Parkhill cleared his throat. " 'Passion,' " he said, regretting his impulsiveness, "is spelled 'p-a-s-s—' "

Before he could complete "passion," the bell rang its reprieve.

The platoon of warriors rose, assembling their effects, streaming to the door, arguing among themselves, calling their familiar salutations. "Good night, all." "A *good* lasson!" "Heppy vik-and." Mr. Trabish, awakened from his slumber, asked, "What happened?"

It had been a difficult evening, Mr. Parkhill thought to himself. A most difficult evening. The road to learning was so long, so hard, strewn with such sunken mines.

He saw Miss Mitnick approach the man who, responsible for all the tumult, had been entirely forgotten in the heat of battle.

"Mr. Pfeiffer," she blushed, "your writing is splendid!"

"Also your sentence structure!" laughed Mr. Nathan.

Mr. Blattberg joined them with a hearty "Pay no attention to cockamamy Keplan!" He twirled his grandsons' baby teeth with zest, and sent Mr. Pfeiffer the half-fraternal, half-subversive smile he employed when trying to recruit allies to the anti-Kaplan forces.

Then, to Mr. Parkhill's astonishment, Mr. Kaplan himself stepped up to Mr. Pfeiffer and extended his hand. "Pfeiffer, I congradulate! I hope you realize I vas only doink mine *duty*. I didn't minn to hoit your fillinks."

"You sabotaged his self-respact!" hissed Mr. Blattberg.

"You made mish-mosh from his recitation!" glared Mr. Olansky.

"You—y-you acted *hard,*" Miss Mitnick stammered.

Mr. Nathan took her hand in his.

But Mr. Pfeiffer straightened his bow tie and said, "If you esk me, Mr. Kaplan wass right."

"*Hanh?*"

"*Who?*"

"*Kep*lan?!" The Blattberg-Mitnick-Olansky task force was flabbergasted.

"A misstake is a misstake," said Fischel Pfeiffer, quoting Mr. Kaplan, indifferent to the coals he was heaping on the heads of his friends. "A fect is also a fect. My pronounssing is a scandal. My mouse is too full 's's.'"

103

"Pfeiffer, dobble congradulations!" cried Mr. Kaplan. "You honist! Batter an honist mistake den a snikky sock-sass! So you made a few mistakes. Who doesn't? Still, you made on me a *fine* imprassion. Soch beauriful hend-writink! Not iven Mitnick or Nat'an P. Nat'an writes so fency. Tell me, vhere you loined how to write like dat?"

"I am in embroidery," preened Mr. Pfeiffer.

"Aha!" Mr. Kaplan beamed. "Vitout men like you vould be a deprassion. . . . Good night, Olansky. Good night, Blatt-boig. Good night, Mitnick." He strode to the door, where he turned, narrowing his eyes as of yore, and in measured cadence murmured, "I vill vipe dat 'Feh!' ot from my mamory, Fischel Pfeiffer. Lat gone-bys be gone-bys! But vun t'ing you should know: You ken write like an angel, you can spall like a profasser, but ve got a *titcher,* Pfeiffer, who, onlass you prononce 'sh' like a mama to a baby an' *not* like you booink at a ballgame, vill hold you in de beginnis' grate if it takes fifty yiss!" He disappeared.

As Mr. Parkhill locked his desk, he had the uneasy feeling that Mr. Kaplan might be right, and hoped against hope that he was wrong. Fifty years . . . ! Unless—yes—*Fata viam invenient.*

104

8

A GLORIOUS PEST

" 'Then, amidst the breathless hush of his peers,' " read Mr. Parkhill, amidst the breathless hush of his flock, " 'Patrick Henry took the floor. All eyes turned to the fiery young lawyer, who proceeded to deliver the most scathing attack on monarchy yet heard in the Virginia House of Burgesses: "Caesar had his Brutus; Charles the First, his Cromwell; and George the Third"—'cries of "Treason! Treason!" interrupted him'—"and George the Third may profit from their example! . . . *If this be treason, make the most of it!*" ' "

Applause rocked the spellbound forum.

"Hooray!" cried Mr. Umea.

"Wonderful!" breathed Miss Mitnick.

"That's the way to talk!" crowed Mr. Nathan.

Mr. Parkhill lowered the book. He felt pleased: not only because the eloquent *démarche* always stirred his senses, but because the beginners' grade, having listened with such intensity of interest, had responded with such amplitude of emotion. "That, class, was one of the most dramatic moments in the history of the thirteen colonies from which our country was formed. And ten years later, this same patriot, Patrick Henry, delivered another speech, which many consider even more memorable. It has, indeed, become one of the truly—er—immortal orations in history." He closed the book. What teacher worth his calling required a text for that matchless peroration? " 'Is life so dear, or peace so sweet, as to be purchased at the price of chains and slavery? Forbid it, Almighty God!' " He paused. " 'I know not what course others may take, but as for me—*give me liberty or give me death!* ' "

If the students had applauded Patrick Henry on monarchy, they brought the rafters down for him on liberty.

"Hoorah!"

"T'ree chiss for Petrick Hanry!"

"Bravo! Bravo!" Lucca Barbella was on his feet, prepared to lead a parade.

"Class . . ."

"Justa like Mazzini!"

"Ha!" Mr. Kaplan's scorn cracked out like lightning. "How you can compare a Petrick Hanry to a—vhat vas dat name you mantioned in de same brat?"

"Giuseppe Mazzini! Greata man! Greata patriot! . . . In Italia, we also have true patriot!"

"Mr. Barbella—"

"If in Italy you had a Petrick Hanry *bifore,* you vouldn't have a Mussolini later!" Mr. Kaplan intoned from on high. He raised his head toward heaven, and declaimed: " 'Give me liberty—or give me dat!' "

"True! True!" cried fierce Hruska.

"Keplen, should go in politics!" Mr. Pinsky slapped his cheek with a resounding "Pssh!"

"This mon—in *politic?!"* Olga Tarnova writhed in nausea.

"Class! Your attention!" Mr. Parkhill was rapping his pointer on the desk without a twinge of uncertainty. (When the tribute due Patrick Henry was being accorded Hyman Kaplan, who had managed to utter the deathless line as if he had made it up on the spot, it was time to call a halt.) "I shall now assign your homework."

106

Out came pencils to record, and notebooks to receive, Mr. Parkhill's instructions.

"During this semester," he began, "we have had occasion to discuss some of the better known episodes in American history. I have not done this in—uh—chronological order, because I have answered your questions as they arose, or explained the background of a holiday as *it* arose. American history, as such, is one of the subjects in Mr. Krout's grade." (He thought it best not to remind them that Mr. Krout was entrenched far beyond the fortress of Miss Higby.) "We discussed Woodrow Wilson, say, before we even *mentioned* the Monroe Doctrine. Or Thomas Paine before one of you brought up Pocahontas."

"I asked about Pocahontas. . . ." murmured "Cookie" Kipnis.

"Y-yes. . . . Well then, your homework assignment is: a composition on any famous figure, or any famous incident, in the American Revolution."

"Foist-cless assignmant!" beamed Mr. Kaplan.

"Hard," said Mr. Wilkomirski.

"Hod but *good!* Who vants an izzy lasson? Izzy is for slowboats."

" 'Slowpokes,' Mr. Kaplan!"

Confusion wracked Mrs. Moskowitz. "Which famous figures? Which accidents?"

" '*In*cidents,' Mrs. Moskowitz, not '*acc*idents'!"

"My mind is a blenk about *in*cidents, also," mourned Mrs. Moskowitz. "Please—a few exemples. . . ."

Stalwarts rushed to help her.

"Try crossing the Delaware!"

"Take Ben Frenklin."

"Liberty Bells."

Mrs. Moskowitz wiped her jowls.

"Maybe the Mayflar!"

"Spilling that tea in Boston Harbra?"

"Don't shoot till their eyes turn white!" sang Mr. Nathan.
Neither heroes, events nor historic sayings sufficed to
lift Mrs. Moskowitz out of gloom's mire.

"Mrs. Moskowitz," Mr. Parkhill began, "I think you
might—"

"Moskovitz, you not tryink!" scowled Mr. Kaplan.

"Vat *am* I doing—ice-skating?" snapped Mrs. Moskowitz.

"You holdink beck de cless!" announced Mr. Kaplan.

"So go witout me!"

"You sebotagink our morals!"

" 'Mor*ale*,' Mr. Kaplan, not '*mo*rals,' " said Mr. Parkhill
anxiously. "Mrs. Moskowitz, the assignment is really not
as hard as you fear. After you get home, when you have
time to think and remember and—review your notes—I'm
sure you will get many ideas." He was not sure Mrs. Moskowitz would get any, much less many, ideas; if an idea
was to inspire Mrs. Moskowitz, it would be because the
idea found a way of seizing her, not the other way around.

Lola Lopez's favorite finger wiggled in the air. "How
long should thees homework last?"

"It should be . . ." Mr. Parkhill weighed his next words
carefully. "I do not want a long or—er—elaborate essay,
class. Let's say—oh, not more than a page and a half. Of
course, one page would do nicely." He hoped he had not
sounded hopeful. "That's all for tonight. . . ."

Four nights later, in the solitude of his apartment, Mr.
Parkhill was correcting their compositions. It was too soon
to know whether he should feel pleased or disappointed.
His students' homework always contained so many *surprises*. Some were heartening, some discouraging, some
paralyzing. This batch of papers contained so many surprises that it was difficult to characterize them at all. The
excursion into history seemed to have carried his pupils
into the most curious *personal* involvements.

Take Mr. Pinsky. Sam Pinsky was an amiable pupil who

never let his reach exceed his grasp. Yet this time, Mr. Pinsky had thrown caution to the winds. He had appraised the entire colonial policy of eighteenth-century England, becoming so incensed by what he called British "cold-heartiness" that he had launched into diatribe:

> Colonists were starving like flys. But all England did was make more taxis. Taxis, taxis, taxis! On food. On tea. Even on a card to a dying mother.
> I think Georgie III was a dummy!

That was not at *all* typical of Mr. Pinsky.

Or take the essay of Stanislaus Wilkomirski, whose ancestors had survived oppressions beside which the Stamp Act could be deemed philanthropic. Mr. Wilkomirski had paid his respects to that peerless seaman, "Admirable Jones." Mr. Parkhill could see how a neophyte might confuse "Admiral" with "admirable," but that Mr. Wilkomirski later alchemized "John Paul Jones" into "Jumpall Jones" Mr. Parkhill found hard to condone.

Or take Mrs. Yanoff. For some reason, the lady in black had taken personal offense at General Cornwallis, scourging him for not surrendering to Washington *soon* enough. Mr. Parkhill could not tell whether Mrs. Yanoff had meant her essay to be descriptive of, or delivered to, contemptible Cornwallis.

Reuben Olansky had penned a tirade against the Tories, whom he accused of crimes too heinous to be described, or, if described, to be spelled correctly. (It was hardly fair to blame the Tories for insulting "prepositions" when all they had done was offer unacceptable propositions.)

After these erratic fulminations, Miss Mitnick's composition was a pleasure to read. Entitled "A Hero: Nathan Hale," her essay contained this moving passage:

> They tied his hands behind to hang him. But brave, with his bare head he made a wonderful statement: "I regret I have only one life to give for the country."

Mr. Hale was not maybe so important as Washington, but he is my hero. I admire.

Why, save for the unfortunate abolition of "admire"'s transitive rights, that paragraph would have done credit to a student in Mrs. O'Hallohan's grade.

Nathan P. Nathan's commendable composition puzzled Mr. Parkhill on one point. The half-page extolled John Hancock, whose handwriting (wrote Mr. Nathan) no red-blooded American would ever "forge." It took quite a few troubling moments before Mr. Parkhill realized that only a "t" separates "forge" from "forget."

Miss Ziev, from whom Mr. Parkhill had not expected to receive any homework at all (Miss Ziev no longer wore the ring given her by Mr. Andrassy), had come through with an unusual offering:

MINUTE MEN

Farm boys with long riffles. Always ready to fight. Did.
A famous battle, with 1 shot the whole world heard, was the Battle of Grand Concourse.

Good work, Minute Men!

The only way Mr. Parkhill could explain how Concord had become "Grand Concourse" was that Miss Ziev had a relative who resided on that thoroughfare.

Mr. Studniczka—Mr. Parkhill sighed. Peter Studniczka had submitted yet another of his cryptic substitutions for prose:

1776

Best Man—G. Washington
Bad Man—King
Trators—Ben and Dick Arnold
Pattriot—*PULASKI FROM POLAND!*

Mr. Parkhill was not happy about that paper. Something in Mr. Studniczka's psychological structure made him approach English vertically. Whether it was because he ac-

110

tually thought in columns (which Mr. Parkhill would understand, were Mr. Studniczka an accountant, or Japanese), or whether he had a phobia about horizontal prose, which requires subject, verb, predicate, Mr. Parkhill did not know. Mr. Studniczka had a long way to go. Mr. Parkhill corrected the spelling of "trators" and "pattriot," and in the margin of Mr. Studniczka's inventory wrote: "This is not a *composition*, Mr. S. Please use whole *sentences!*" He started to put the paper aside, paused, and added: "Bene*dict* Arnold. One traitor, not two."

The next paper popped pellets of color before Mr. Parkhill's eyes.

<u>AL X. HAMILTON VERSES TOM S. JEFFERSON</u>
A Play!
By
H*Y*M*A*N K*A*P*L*A*N

Mr. Parkhill put the paper down and went into the kitchen for a glass of water. He sharpened his red marking pencil thoughtfully before picking up Mr. Kaplan's "A Play!" again. Before he had read two lines, he was wincing.

HAMILTON: "The government should be strong!"
JEFFERSON: "No! Be ware strong government. People must decide."
HAMILTON: "People? Ha, ha, ha, ha. Don't trust people."
JEFFERSON: "I TRUST! Also U.S. money says 'God trusts.' O.K. *How's about you?*"
HAMILTON: "You are a dreamy. Don't be so nave."

At this point, Mr. Kaplan, exhausted by the weight of long words, had dropped into abbreviations; this had no doubt lessened the strain on his fingers but played havoc with the names of his protagonists:

HAM: "Every business needs a boss!"
JEFF: "From bosses comes Kings! Don't forget!"

111

HAM: "That's my last offer, Tom S. Jefferson!"
JEFF: "Same to you, Al X. Hamilton."

Mr. Parkhill reached for an aspirin.

"Good evening, class," said Mr. Parkhill. "First, I shall return your homework. Each paper has been corrected and—evaluated. Please study my comments—they are in red—carefully. I believe you can learn more from your own mistakes than from almost any other—"

Up stabbed Mr. Kaplan's hand.

"Y-yes?"

"You *liked* de homevoik, Mr. Pockheel?"

"Well," the reply unrolled cautiously, "I think all of you *tried* very hard. There were, of course, errors, many errors —in some cases, too many. I shall now distribute—"

"Still, *som* homevoik gave you a big soprise?"

Mr. Parkhill averted his gaze. He knew exactly what Mr. Kaplan was driving at. The man was trying to lure Mr. Parkhill into some compliment—say, that imagination is more important than error, and that one particular student had by sheer inspiration soared far, far above his fellows. . . . "Mr. Kaplan," said Mr. Parkhill firmly, "the purpose of homework is not to—'surprise.' In fact, the best homework is the kind that contains no errors at all, thus giving me no 'surprises.' " With that *tu quoque,* Mr. Parkhill distributed the homework. "Miss Atrakian . . . Mr. Olansky . . ."

Mr. Kaplan looked crestfallen. How, looking crestfallen, he exuded the pride of one who had scaled Parnassus, Mr. Parkhill would never understand.

". . . C. J. Fledermann."

The compositions streamed back to their creators, whose swift sounds of illumination rewarded Mr. Parkhill.

"I spalled wrong 'Philadelphia'!"

"Harry is not 'Hairy' . . ."

"Psssh! Was I wrong!" Mr. Pinsky's self-administered slap told Mr. Parkhill that Mr. Pinsky was determined to learn, whatever the emotional cost.

"Examine the corrections carefully, class. If you have a question, just raise your hand. . . ." He strolled down the aisle. (There is a world of difference, Mr. Parkhill had learned, between sitting at a desk and strolling down an aisle: the former is judiciary, the latter egalitarian; the one stresses decorum, the other induces relaxation.)

The next hour went so swiftly that the bell rang before anyone suspected it was time for recess.

In the final portion of the session, Mr. Parkhill conducted a spelling drill of which he felt rather proud: twenty words containing "e-i-g-h-t" (from "freight" to "weight" via "height"), and twenty containing "o-u-g-h" (from "cough" through "rough" to "trough").

He had just announced "Bought . . . thought . . . enough . . ." when Mrs. Moskowitz flung down her pen and appealed to Miss Kipnis beside her: " 'Enough'? *Enough!* Why not put in 'f' when is pro*noun*ced 'ffff'? A mind can creck from soch torture, Cookie!"

"You got to be patient," sighed Miss Kipnis.

"Don't give op!" called Rochelle Goldberg, placating her own nerves with a caramel. "Learning takes *time*. . . ."

They had reckoned without the defender of the faith. "Ha! Vhat kind students are talkink? Moskovitz," called Mr. Kaplan, "U.S. vasn't fonded by sissies!"

"I dun't want to found, I want to spall!"

"Class—"

"Nottink good is izzy!" declaimed Hyman Kaplan. *"Eating* is good, and easy!"

"You compare spallink to eatink?" Mr. Kaplan's expres-

113

sion set a new high for amazement. "You tritt English like lemb chops?"

"You make English chop suey!" jeered Mr. Olansky.

His cohorts burst into laughter.

"Class, *class,*" said Mr. Parkhill. (Mr. Nathan was choking.) "We are engaged in a spelling drill, not a debate!" He waited for combat to subside, then addressed Mrs. Moskowitz. "I can well understand how someone from another land feels when confronted by some of the peculiar ways in which English words are spelled."

"I am from anodder lend," said Mr. Kaplan, "an' still I don't holler 'Halp!'"

"Mr. Kaplan," said Mr. Parkhill crisply, "English *is* a difficult language. And many of our words *are* spelled in most unreasonable—"

"Moskovitz ken still make a good profit from odder pipple's semples!" intoned Hyman Kaplan.

Mr. Parkhill frowned. "I beg your pardon?"

Mr. Kaplan sat as serene as a lamb.

"I thought I heard you say that Mrs. Moskowitz could—er—'make a good profit'—"

"Like de Pilgrim's Fodder," said Mr. Kaplan.

"The Pilgri*m* Father*s*!" Mr. Parkhill tried not to sound annoyed.

"What have the Pilgrims to do with Mrs. Moskowitz?" protested Miss Mitnick.

"Yos!"

"Tell!"

"It's obvious," said Mr. Kaplan carelessly. Apparently, he considered it too obvious to continue.

"Mr. Kaplan," said Mr. Parkhill, "your comment is as unclear to me as it is to Miss Mitnick! I suggest you explain —no, no, you need not go to the *front*—"

Mr. Kaplan was already halfway to the podium he adored. There he stopped, turned, and withered Mrs. Moskowitz with his scorn. "De Pilgrim's Fodder—"

"Pilgri*m* Father*s!*"

"—didn't sail beck to England becawss dey had to spall de void 'enough'!" Now the patriot transferred his attention to Miss Mitnick. "Dey had beeger trobbles. Hindians, messecres, skinny hovests—"

"Mr. Kap—"

"—spying fromm de Franch, poisicutions fromm de British—"

"Stop with the lecture in American history!" howled Mr. Olansky.

"Stick to Mrs. Moskowitz!" shouted Mr. Blattberg.

"Class—"

"The Pilgrim Fothahs didn't hov to put op with Koplon!" lowed Olga Tarnova.

Triton was deaf to the minnows. "An' vhen de time came for de Amarican Ravolution, brave men like John Edems, Tom Spain—"

"Thomas *Paine,* not 'Spain'—"

"—knew dey had missink a slogan, a spok, a fire to light de lemps of Liberty! So along came Pettereck Hanry."

"It's *'Pat*rick,' not 'Pett*e*rick'—and 'H*e*nry,' not 'H*a*nry.' "

Mr. Kaplan's gaze had gone dreamy. "Dat vas a man . . . A prince! A tong like silver."

"Mr. Kaplan, it's 'tongue,' not 'tong'!"

"So *Pat*rick Hanry vent into de Virginia House of Poichases—"

" 'Burgess—' "

"—an' at vunce all vas qviet, like de gomment districk on Chrissmis Iv. So Patrick Hanry got don on de floor—"

"Took the floor!" Mr. Parkhill was beginning to feel dehydrated.

"—took de floor, an' in dose beauriful, parful voids vhich comm don de santuries for all Amaricans who got true blood—"

" 'True-*blooded'*—"

"—Pet sad, 'Julius Scissor had his Buddhist—'"

"'*Brutus'!*" cried Mr. Parkhill.

"'Cholly de Foist had his Cronvall, an' if crazy King Judge got a brain in his had he *vill make a profit from soch a semple!*'"

Mr. Parkhill sank into his seat, which seemed to have had its legs shortened.

"Dat," Mr. Kaplan concluded, "also epplies to Moskovitz!" He strode back to his chair.

"All I said was 'enough' should have vun little 'f'!" wailed Mrs. Moskowitz.

"Koplen, you mad!" fumed Olaf Umea.

"Give an *inch*, Mr. Kaplan—"

"Thees mon will change heestory single-honded!" That, perhaps the truest thought yet uttered, came from Lola Lopez.

"Call a doctor! Examine his head!" Mr. Olansky had placed his own head between his hands.

"Mr. *Kap*lan—" Mr. Parkhill began. But he scarcely knew where to begin, so he began again. "Mr. Kaplan, rarely have I heard so many mispronunciations in so short a time! Charles the First was *not* 'Charley the—er—Foist.' Cromwell was *not* 'Cronvall.' And what Patrick Henry said was certainly *not* what you said he said! There is a world of difference, Mr. Kaplan, between 'George the Third *may profit from their example*' and 'George the Third can make a profit out of such a sample'! Do you understand?"

Mr. Nathan was gasping and laughing in tandem.

Mr. Kaplan had cocked his head to one side, signifying attention, closed both eyes, indicating cerebration, then opened one eye, denoting illumination. "Yes, sir. But I vill alvays edmire de glorious pest."

"Mistake!" sang out Miss Mitnick. "'*Past*' is not '*pest.*'"

One Mr. Wodjik guffawed. The other Mr. Wodjik gig-

116

gled. Miss Goldberg swallowed a Kiss from Hershey, Pa.

"Tonight is averybody an axpert?" Mr. Kaplan caustically inquired.

"Tonight," Miss Mitnick retorted, "you don't have to be an expert to know the *'past'* from a *'pest'!*"

The room rocked with merriment.

"Good for you, Miss Mitnick!"

"Bravissima!"

"This time Rose has him in a coroner!" exulted Mr. Nathan.

Mr. Kaplan ignored the petty barbs and puny arrows, turning to the one who had given him the challenge direct. "Mitnick," he said with pious pity, *"you* are talking abot prononcing; but *I* am talking abot history!"

" 'Past' *means* history!" Miss Mitnick blushed tearfully. "What you said was 'the glorious p*e*st.' "

"Koplen, give up!" advised C. J. Fledermann.

"Keplan, sit down!" brayed Miss Pomeranz.

"Kaplen, give an *inch!*" pleaded Bessie Shimmelfarb.

"Mr. Kaplan," cut in Mr. Parkhill. "Miss Mitnick is absolutely right! 'Past' refers to what has gone by. 'P*e*st,' on the other hand, refers to an annoying or irritat—" Too late, too late did Mr. Parkhill see the trap into which he, like poor Miss Mitnick, had fallen.

"To a tyrent like King Judge Number T'ree," declaimed Hyman Kaplan, "vhat else vas Patrick Hanry axcept a glorious pest?"

After that, twenty words with "o-u-g-h" seemed inglorious trivia.

9

BRIEF BUDDHA

No trumpets blared as the fat little man marched into the room. He was moonfaced and ruddy. His nose was tiny, his mustache reddish. The mustache was so thick it made the nose resemble a grape.

The little man reminded Mr. Parkhill of a Buddha. Buddhas, of course, do not wear mustaches; they look supremely serene, ever-so-wise, and rather jolly: this stranger radiated the gaiety of a radish. Still, he made Mr. Parkhill think of a Buddha. . . .

The stranger halted before Mr. Parkhill's desk. His left arm cradled a derby as if it was a baby. His right arm stiffened as, without a word, he thrust forth a yellow card:

VISITOR'S PASS

AMERICAN NIGHT PREPARATORY SCHOOL

FOR ADULTS

Please admit bearer: *Mr. Teitelman*
for one trial lesson.

> *Leland Robinson*
> Principal
> by *M. S.*

The names were written in on the printed form, in the unmistakable scrawl of Miss Schnepfe, Mr. Robinson's factotem. Miss Schnepfe's first name was Louella, but she had fallen into the habit of signing herself "Miss S." When she was in a hurry, as she must have been in the case above, she initialed things "M. S." (Several members of the A.N.P.S.A. faculty felt that power had gone to Miss Schnepfe's head.)

As Mr. Parkhill deciphered the visitor's name on the yellow card, the entire beginners' grade appraised its prospective colleague: Rochelle Goldberg with the thirst of a maiden approaching thirty, Mr. Blattberg with the suspicion of a bill collector, Mrs. Yanoff with the expertise acquired in her search for a mate for her daughter.

"Mr.—er—Teitelman?" smiled Mr. Parkhill.

The fat little man drooped. He did not seem optimistic.

"Take a seat, please . . . anywhere." Mr. Parkhill kept smiling, for he knew how self-conscious a newcomer is. "And please consider yourself a full-fledged member of the class for the evening. Enter into our work just as if you were a regular student. . . . Indeed, I hope you *will* be, after tonight." Mr. Parkhill pumped fresh air into his smile, but not a flicker of pleasure lightened the dour countenance. The fat little man merely trudged to the first empty chair he beheld; it was in the front row. This caused considerable stirrings and murmurs amongst his peers, for new students, and certainly *visitors,* invariably sought a haven in the last row. But the stranger plumped his pudgy form into that vacant chair in the front line, between Mrs. Pilpul, on his left, and Hyman Kaplan, on his right.

Mr. Parkhill announced: "Tonight, we shall devote the first half of our session to completing the Recitation and Speech exercise of last evening. We still have to hear from —let me see"—he consulted the class roll—"Mr. Hruska, Miss Atrakian, Mrs. Moskowitz, and—yes, Mr. Trabish."

Three of the four sentenced to oratory promptly moaned.

"I'll be tarrible," soughed Mr. Hruska.

119

Miss Atrakian wet her lips nervously. "I wish I don't have to go."

Mr. Trabish made neither sound nor sigh, until the "Oy" from Mrs. Moskowitz roused him from slumber. "Time to go home?" he blinked.

"Time to vake op!" said Mr. Kaplan.

"We shall give our speakers a few moments to review their remarks," announced Mr. Parkhill brightly. "Meanwhile, the rest of the class might brush up on page forty-six of our textbook."

The congregation rustled through *English for Beginners.* Page 46 contained a list of transitive verbs. Dark scowls and glum mutters ascended from the ranks. The beginners' grade *hated* transitive verbs; they resented the hard-and-fast rule that transitive verbs require a definite object. (Mr. Kaplan had once complained, "I ken be dafinite mit*out* an objeck.")

Mr. Parkhill turned to the fat little man. "You may share page forty-six with Mrs. Pilpul. . . ."

The widow Pilpul pushed *English for Beginners* to her right with flirtatious intimations. But the roly-poly guest made no reactive lean to his left. His thoughts were obviously elsewhere; his gaze was fixed glassily on some ogre above Mr. Parkhill's head.

Meanwhile, the four scholars assigned to recite conducted individual rites of preparation. Miss Atrakian opened and closed her notebook—whispering a line with the book closed, opening it to check on memory, closing the book, mumbling the next line of her speech, reopening the book. . . . Vasil Hruska, who was made of sterner stuff, shunned unworthy cues and props; he rehearsed his address in silent mouthings. Mrs. Moskowitz tried to mollify fate by wailing "I'll be a dummy!" And the last member of the quartet, Mr. Trabish, began to rub his hands. (Mr. Trabish's years as a baker had taught him to clear his mind by massaging his palms.)

To all these preliminary orisons, Hyman Kaplan paid not the slightest attention. He was absorbed in assessing the fat little man out of the corner of one eye; his other eye remained fixed on Mr. Parkhill, like a sentry. (Mr. Kaplan appeared to possess a separate guidance system for each orb; it was uncanny.) For several long moments Mr. Kaplan subjected the rotund visitor to optic synopsis. Would the stranger prove brilliant or stupid? Would he speed up or drag down the sacred transmission of knowledge? Above all, would he be friend or foe? (Neutrality, to Mr. Kaplan, was inconceivable.)

Mr. Kaplan finally leaned leftward and, in a confidential tone, whispered: "How's by you de name, plizz?"

The newcomer twitched, but said nothing.

Mr. Kaplan cleared his throat. "Eh . . . How—is—by—you —de *name?*"

Buddha blinked, reached into his vest, and placed an impressive fountain pen on the arm of his chair. A name, stamped in gold, glittered on the barrel of the pen.

" 'F. Teitelman,' " Mr. Kaplan read. " 'F'—aha! For 'Philip.' "

The mustache quivered in the negative.

"Not for 'Philip'?" Mr. Kaplan pondered the duplicity of 'F.' "Aha! 'Frenk'!"

The nose above the mustache rejected "Frenk."

"Eh—so vat *is* by you de name?"

"Jerome."

" *'Jerome'?* But dat's mit a 'G'! So vhy is on your fontain pan 'F'?!"

The dumpling grunted, "It belongs to my wife."

"My!" murmured Mr. Kaplan.

Mrs. Pilpul's countenance darkened.

"Well, class!" Mr. Parkhill tore his attention away from the little drama which had held him in thrall. "We should be ready now. Mrs. Moskowitz, will you please recite first?"

The portly matron rose, froze, recovered, stepped on Mr.

Fledermann's shoe, blubbered remorse, tugged at her girdle, bobbled her purse, returned Miss Mitnick's encouraging smile with a Cheyne-Stokes rattle—all in the time it took her to lumber from the row in the back to the platform at the front.

"Now, you'll gonna hear mistakes!" Mr. Kaplan grinned to the fat little man. "By de bushel!"

Mr. Nussbaum, who was endowed with exceptional hearing, snapped, "They should hire you for Yom Kippur!"

"Truth is batter than veseline," rejoined Mr. Kaplan.

"You smesh a poisson's confidence!" charged Miss Kipnis.

"How ken you smesh vhat *isn't?*"

"Class!" called Mr. Parkhill. "This is no way to start off! I *must* ask for—silence. Mrs. Moskowitz, state the subject of your recitation, please."

Mrs. Moskowitz, who had been in no condition to hear Mr. Kaplan's prophecy, wiped the perspiration off her brow. "My sobject is—'Arond My Flet.'" (Mrs. Moskowitz had become fixated, in her orations, on the familiar terrain of her apartment: "Getting a New Carpet," "Cleaning Drapes," "Cooking Big Meals." Once, in reckless expansion, she had expatiated on "In a Kitchen Is Gaz a Danger!!") "Men don't know how hard is life for ladies! Housewoik is hodder than homewoik. Also hodder than being in a factory or stending behind a conter." She stopped. "Hommeny mistakes so far?"

"Not so many," smiled Mr. Parkhill. "You might be a *bit* more careful in pronunciation. It's *'hard*er,' for example, not *'hod*der.' And—a mistake many of you make—*'work,'* not *'woik.'*"

"*Soch* a titcher ve got." Mr. Kaplan beamed at the fat little man; the freshman's features remained as unanimated as farina.

"Go on, Mrs. Moskowitz."

The dowager swallowed air and, bosom heaving, declaimed: "Ladies work in a shop or store all day, but still, on coming home, don't rast! They have to clinn up de house, make sopper, take care of children (if there are, which I have, two, long should they live and be halthy), then get for tomorrow morning brakfast raddy, do laundry, fix clothes, or—or—" The prolonged passage had exhausted Mrs. Moskowitz's resources. "—and so far!" She stopped.

Mr. Parkhill sent her an invigorating nod.

Mrs. Moskowitz flailed her hands. "So what more is to *tell?*"

"Abot feexing claws!" trumpeted Mr. Kaplan.

"Awright," said Mrs. Moskowitz, startled by the source of assistance. "I'll describe fixing clothes."

"Teitelman," Mr. Kaplan whispered, "don't be a shy. You ken give ideas, too!"

The sphinx sat inscrutable.

"For fixing clothes," announced Mrs. Moskowitz, "you should have a niddle, a spool of trad the same color, and also a little—"

"Time!" called the stranger.

All heads swung in surprise. Visitors *never* volunteered suggestions.

"Fine, Teitelman!" chortled Mr. Kaplan. "Dat's a boy!"

But Mrs. Moskowitz stared at the interloper with animus. "Why *time,* Mr. New? For fixing clothes you should have a niddle, som trad—"

"You nid time *also!*" Mr. Kaplan defended his protégé.

"And you also nidd a *chair,* for sitting on," shouted Mrs. Moskowitz, "and *light,* you should see, and a *roof* you shouldn't get vet! *Time?!*" she repeated hotly. "I want to tell about mending socks and shoits, and Mr. Mustache dregs in a clock!"

"You right!" called Mr. Tomas Wodjik.

"Good for you!" chimed in Milas Wodjik.

"Kaplan, sharup!" scowled Mr. Olansky.

Mr. Parkhill had been tapping his ruler on the desk for five seconds. "Class . . . *class*. . . . Our visitor simply offered —a suggestion. Proceed, Mrs. Moskowitz."

"So like I said," the aggrieved one continued, "for sewing, you should have a niddle, some trad—and something else. Because if you have a very *tick* piece goods, like a man's coat, how can you push t'rough a niddle?! So you have to put on your pushing finger a tiny, teeny cop. From tin it's made, full of small bumps, so the niddle shouldn't slip. It's called a—"

"Dumbbell," sang Buddha.

Some gasped, some goggled, some winced, but Mrs. Moskowitz snapped, "Mister-New-Student, I-don't-know-who-you-are—"

"De name is Teitelman," beamed Mr. Kaplan.

"—*I* don't mean 'dumbbell'! Maybe *your* vife uses dumbbells for sewing. *I* use a *t'imble!* Now if butt-in Mr. Teitelbum—"

"Teitel*man,*" said Mr. Kaplan.

"—stops intropting, I'll go on. . . . If you have a niddle and trad and *t'imble,* the rast is easy. You just fill op de holes."

"Bravo!" rejoiced Mr. Barbella.

"Congradzulazion!" cracked Mr. Wilkomirski.

Mrs. Moskowitz, breathing heavily, ran two fingers through her hair. "So what *else?*"

"How about washing floors?" prompted Mr. Blattberg.

"Clean your windolls," offered Goldie Pomeranz.

"Wex the tables," hinted a cabinetmaker.

But Mrs. Moskowitz, unable to both think and hearken simultaneously, plumbed her own soul. "Cooking! Yas! Arond every lady's home is cooking! Which I love. Since I am a little girl, I am cooking. And baking . . . Baking! Oh, I—love—baking! I bake brat, rolls, cookies, even—"

"Pies," called Mr. Teitelman.

"CAKE!" shouted Mrs. Moskowitz. "Not *pies!* Cake! 'K-A-K-E'!"

"Mrs. Moskowitz, it's 'c-a-' "

Mr. Kaplan rushed to protect the flank of his ward. "But you make pies *too,* no, Moskovitz?"

"I—bake—CAKE!"

"Moskovitz, you too axcited!"

"Mr. Kap—"

"I bake *cake!*"

"A foist-cless cook got to make pies!"

"Corract!" concurred Mr. Trabish.

"Who asked you?!" snapped Mrs. Moskowitz.

"He's a *b*aker!" cried Mr. Kaplan.

"Class—"

"And Mr. New? He's a Franch chaff?" flared the matron. "Teitelman vas only tryink to halp!"

"Mr. Kap—"

"Let Mr. Mustache halp *you!*" fumed Mrs. Moskowitz. *"Me* he'll drive crazy—"

"Mrs. Mosko—"

"—giving dumbbells for t'imbles, dregging in *time* all of a sodden, den t'rowing *pies* in my cake! Enoff! I'll *bust!* Good-bye!" And with that, cheeks aflame, her hair so disarranged she looked like a frantic Medusa, Sadie Moskowitz stomped back to her chair.

The sensitive tribunal seethed—with sympathy for Mrs. Moskowitz and sneers to tactless Teitelman.

"He didn't give Mrs. M. a chonce!" moaned Olga Tarnova.

"He was trying to halp!" Mr. Pinsky echoed his master.

"Help?" railed Christian Fledermann. "Zoch help iss poison!"

"I hear bees in de room agan," murmured Mr. Kaplan.

"Please . . . *class!*" Mr. Parkhill marshaled all his powers of conciliation to head off open warfare. "I *do* think Mr. Teitelman was just trying to—participate in our—"

"Soitinly!" said Mr. Kaplan.

"A new student we shouldn't poisicute," observed "Cookie" Kipnis.

"Who *pois*icuted?" flared Mr. Blattberg. *"He* was the one—"

"Class—"

"In my opinion," called Mrs. Pilpul, whose opinion no one ever solicited, "Mr. Teitelman should get a pinch sympaty."

"He should have his lips sewed up!" rejoined Mr. Olansky.

In vain did Mr. Parkhill tap his knuckles on the desk, in vain seek a truce. "Class, this is ab—"

"Everyone has right to correct," muttered Mr. Studniczka.

"But not to neg, neg, *neg* a spiker," returned Mrs. Yanoff.

"I *admire* a new man who talks his *foist time in class!*" declared Mrs. Shimmelfarb.

"I odmire a mon which knows the difference of cake and pie!" retorted Olga Tarnova.

"That will be enough!" Mr. Parkhill's severe tone squelched the broil and brabble. "Mrs. Moskowitz, I'm sure we all understand how you feel. But Mr. Teitelman is—" He might have been shooting peas at Gibraltar.

"Mr. Mustache is anodder Kaplin!" cried Mrs. Moskowitz.

"Class—"

"I suggest Kaplen *and* his pel sharop!" huffed Mr. Nussbaum, through quivering whiskers.

"I soggest you stop a vulgar word like 'Sharop'!" exclaimed Shirley Ziev.

Throughout the clash and conflict, Messrs. Kaplan and Teitelman sat quiet, side by side, comrades indifferent to snipers. They paid scant attention to the next speech, by Miss Atrakian. They raised no quibbles about the oration of Mr. Hruska. They nodded absently to the words of Mr. Trabish, who had been the first to rally to their standard. The two knights just reposed in valor, bound by fraternal effort in a noble cause.

When the recess bell tolled, the chattering class started into the corridor.

Mr. Kaplan smiled at the fat little man. "You vant to stap otside a few minutes?"

The orphan of the storm shook his head.

"Hau Kay," said Mr. Kaplan. "Stay. Rast. T'ink op more fine ideas!" He headed for the throng beyond the door, gloating.

The fat little man sat quite still in his chair, gazing at Mr. Parkhill. Only the two of them were in the room.

Mr. Parkhill cleared his throat. He wanted to tell Mr. Teitelman that class sessions were not usually so agitated; that emotions had been roused to such a pitch because of the class's genuine thirst for knowledge; that there was, in fact, a certain value in heated debate. . . . Before Mr. Parkhill could phrase even the first of these propitiations, the visitor stood up, placed his derby upon his head, said "Goom-bye," and waddled out of the room.

Mr. Parkhill looked after him in distress.

Soon the gong sounded an end to recess. The scholars filed in. They took their places. Mr. Kaplan did not sit down. "Teitelman?" he called. His eyes darted right and left. "Who seen Teitelman?"

No one had seen Teitelman. No one seemed to know where or how the fat little man had vanished. (Mr. Parkhill wondered whether Buddha had ever used a Fire Exit.)

"Let us take up the list of transitive verbs on page forty-six," said Mr. Parkhill.

The textbooks rustled busily.

"Miss Goldberg, will you begin?"

Miss Goldberg read: "Tell . . . give . . . throw."

The hateful verbs stilled the last perturbations of the beginners' grade.

"Remove . . . choose . . . catch . . ." read Mr. Wodjik. (Since they often changed places, Mr. Parkhill was not sure which Mr. Wodjik it was.)

Heads bobbed up and down in rhythm to the litany. All heads, that is, save Hyman Kaplan's. He was inert, gloom drowning his usual vivacity. He ignored the travail of the transitive. He uttered not one "My!" or "Aha!" to verbs passive. The heart had gone out of Hyman Kaplan. Lost was the old bravado, gone the bright, irrepressible flair.

Only once did Mr. Kaplan emerge from the gorge of mourning. That was when, assessing the empty chair beside him, Mr. Kaplan sighed, "My . . . I lost a *fine* frant."

10

THE PERILS OF LOGIC

In the beginning, Mr. Parkhill had assumed that the incredible things Mr. Kaplan did to the English language were the offshoots of ignorance—ignorance garnished with originality, to be sure, but ignorance nonetheless. (How else explain Mr. Kaplan's belief that a summary is a short summer?)

But then Mr. Parkhill began to think that it wasn't ignorance which governed Mr. Kaplan so much as *impulsiveness*. (That would explain the sentence he concocted when asked to use the word "orchard": "Each Sunday he sent her a dozen orchards.") And for a time Mr. Parkhill toyed with the notion that Mr. Kaplan's startling improvisations were produced by a certain mischievousness. (How else account for the man's blithe assertion that the body of water which separates France from Britain is "the English Canal"?)

But all of these hypotheses collapsed the night the beginners' grade was running through a lively exercise on synonyms and antonyms. Mr. Kaplan placed these sets of "opposites" on the board:

slow	fast
upton	donton
rich	skinny

Most teachers would have dismissed "skinny" as a grotesque guess. But Mr. Parkhill thought it over with great

129

care. *Why,* he asked himself, would an intelligent man like Mr. Kaplan consider "skinny" the opposite of "rich"? The answer came to him in a flash: the reason Mr. Kaplan thought "skinny" the antonym of "rich" was that in his experience rich people were fat! *Ergo:* if the rich are fat, then *(mutatis mutandis)* the poor must be skinny. (He wished Mr. Kaplan had used "thin" instead of "skinny," but he had to admit that "skinny" is much more graphic.)

The more Mr. Parkhill analyzed Mr. Kaplan's peculiar solecisms the more did he become convinced that neither ignorance nor caprice nor puckishness was the key to Mr. Kaplan's airy revision of the English language. It was logic. A private kind of logic. A unique logic. A secret, baffling logic. But logic. Mr. Kaplan made mistakes because he simply ignored or refused to abide by convention. After all, human conventions do not rest on reason, but on consensus. Mr. Kaplan's malapropisms therefore arose from the fact that his logic and the logic of English just did not happen to coincide! (Mr. Parkhill had always been a staunch believer in *"De gustibus non est disputandum."*)

Any lingering doubts Mr. Parkhill harbored about the whole problem vanished when Mr. Kaplan called the instrument which doctors use to listen to the human heart a "deathascope."

One Wednesday night Mr. Parkhill gained a fresh insight into the workings of Mr. Kaplan's mind. Miss Goldie Pomeranz was reciting, recounting a frightening experience with a dog. The dog's name, according to Miss Pomeranz, was "Rax." (She probably meant "Rex"; Mr. Parkhill had never heard of a dog named "Rax.")

"Was he a wild bist!" Miss Pomeranz declaimed. "I was trying to pat him, very nice, on the head. And I was saying, 'Here, Rax, be a good boy.' And without a word, not even one bow-wow or groll or making angry his tail, Rax bite me in the lag!"

" 'Bite,' " said Mr. Parkhill, "is the *present* tense, Miss Pomeranz."

Chagrin clouded the bitten maid's countenance.

"You want the—*past* tense," Mr. Parkhill said gently. "What is the past tense of 'to bite'?"

"Omigod," bleated Miss Pomeranz.

"The past tense of 'to bite'—anyone?"

Mr. Kaplan sent up a trial balloon: "Is it 'bited' . . . ?"

"No, it is not 'bited'!"

"I agree," said Mr. Kaplan.

Miss Mitnick raised her hand, just above the head of Mr. Trabish, dozing pleasantly in the row ahead. "The past tense of 'bite,' " she volunteered, "is 'bit.' "

"Right, Miss Mitnick! 'Bite, bit.' The dog *bit* you in the leg, Miss Pomeranz. And the past participle—?"

" 'Bitten,' " blushed Rose Mitnick.

Nathan P. Nathan applauded.

But Mr. Kaplan closed one eye, cocked his head, and whispered to himself, "Mitnick gives 'bit' . . . *'Bit'* Mitnick gives? Also 'bitten' . . . ?! 'Bite, bit, *bitten'*—it sonds awful fonny."

Mr. Parkhill could not pretend he had not heard this soliloquy: the entire room had heard it. "Er—isn't that clear, Mr. Kaplan?"

"Clear, Mr. Pockheel?" The ruminating orb opened. "Yas, sir. But I don't see *why* it should be 'bitten.' . . . To me, it don't make *sense."* (Yes, he had said "why," not "vhy.")

"It *doesn't* make sense?" Mr. Parkhill echoed lamely, then glimpsed a golden opportunity: "You mean it isn't *logical?"*

"Pretzicely."

"Well, Mr. Kaplan! Let us address ourselves directly to that point! Language is not always—logical. But it has *laws,* laws which have grown and become accepted down the centuries." Mr. Parkhill was rather excited by the

131

chance to enlighten the class on so important a concept. "I'm sure you remember our various verb drills, Mr. Kaplan. Well, the verb 'to bite' is very much like, say, the verb 'to hide.' 'To hide' is conjugated 'hide, hid, hidden.' Why, then, isn't it—er—logical for the principal parts of 'to bite' to be 'bite, bit, bitten'?"

Mr. Kaplan hesitated but a smidgeon of a moment. "I t'ink de past time of 'bite' should be 'bote.' "

" 'Bote'?" Mr. Parkhill echoed.

" 'Bote.' Because, if it is 'write, wrote, written,' why not 'bite, bote, bitten'?"

Mr. Nathan laughed until the tears rolled down his cheeks. Mr. Barbella hooted.

Mr. Parkhill wished he could lie down.

"B-but there is not such a *word* as 'bote'!" cried Miss Mitnick.

" 'Not such a woid,' " Mr. Kaplan echoed, all pity. "Mine dear Mitnick, did I say dere *is* such a woid? Never! All I said is: why *shouldn't* be such a woid?!"

"Mr. Kaplan, *there is no such word,* as Miss Mitnick quite correctly observed!" Poor Miss Mitnick was biting her lips. "Nor is it 'logical' that there *should* be such a word!" This time Mr. Parkhill was determined to nip the Kaplan casuistry in the bud. He recapitulated the exercise on regular and irregular verbs. He recited the principal parts of a dozen samples. He spoke with special earnestness, for he suspected that a good deal depended on his exposition.

By the time Mr. Parkhill had finished, Mr. Kaplan was all admiration, Miss Mitnick's normal pallor had returned, Mr. Olansky smirked like a crocodile, and Miss Goldberg savored a gumdrop.

Recitation and Speech continued: Mr. Sam Pinsky delivered a brief address on the mysteries of his craft, pressing. Mrs. Pilpul followed with an eyewitness account of an altercation in a "beauty saloon." Mr. Trabish, energized by brief slumber, issued an apologia for the community of bakers, who are as fallible as any other caste of men, and confessed that on at least two occasions he had carelessly produced soggy hard "rawls." Mrs. Yanoff, her black dress shining, described a trip she and her "husbar," Morris, were hoping to make to a metropolis called "Spittsburgh." The recess bell quelled the skirmish over "husbar" and the brouhaha about "Spittsburgh."

The second student to take the floor after the session resumed was Hyman Kaplan. "Ladies, gantleman, *patient* Mr. Pockheel. . . . Tonight, I'll gonna talk abot noose-peppers, dose vunderful, movvelous—"

"Pardon me," Mr. Parkhill broke in at once. (It was fool-hardy to give Mr. Kaplan free rein at the very outset of what was going to be an elegy to journalism.) "It's 'Tonight I am going'—not 'I'll gonna'—'to talk.' . . . And the word is *'newspapers,'* not 'noose-peppers.'" Briskly, he printed NOOSE, PEPPER, and NEWSPAPER on the board. Carefully, he explained the meaning of each word. (When he drove home the difference between "news" and "noose," Mr. Blattberg burst into cackling.)

"So," Mr. Kaplan resumed his tale, "a *news*paper is to me a *miracle* we have in tsivilization. What is a *news*paper? Ha! It's a show! It's education! It's tregedy! It's comical! It's movvelous! A *news*paper gives to our messes—"

" 'Mass*es*,' Mr. Kaplan, not 'mess*es*'!"

"—gives to our *mass*es information about de whole woild. Even advoitismants in a paper titch a lesson. An' ufcawss all odder pots of a paper: de hatlininks—"

"*Mr.* Kaplan! Headlines are *not* 'hatlinings.'"

"Denk you. Also editorials, cottoons—"

" 'Cartoons'—"

"—an' pictchiss. In *news*papers we find ot all dat's happenink at home an' aboard."

" 'A*broad*'! And it's good to hear 'what' and 'we'!"

"—An' *abroad*. . . . We read abot politic, abot crimes, abot all kinds *scendels* people are making—" Mr. Kaplan paused to cluck sorrow for the persistent follies of the human race. "Also a paper gives *useful* inflamation: stock mockit prices, where a show is playink in case you want to spand a fortune to go look on it, who died, who got marry—" He shot a congratulatory nod toward Miss Ziev (who, after so on-and-off a betrothal, was about to become Mrs. Andrassy) and encouraging winks to both Miss Mitnick and Nathan P. Nathan (who had not resolved the conflict between surrendering his freedom or his basketball). "Also we get wather raports, abot if it is going to be sun, snow or rain. . . . Well, dis morning I was reading a newspaper. In English!" Mr. Kaplan paused, should his colleagues care to acclaim this feat. "I rad abot de naxt elaction. So what de paper said? Foist, he said dat de—"

"Mr. Kaplan, one moment! It's *'it* said,' for a newspaper, not *'he* said.' "

Mr. Kaplan looked stunned. "Not 'he'?"

"No, of course not 'he.' *'It.'* Have you forgotten our lesson on pronouns? On gender? 'He' is masculine, 'she' is feminine. Not that grammatical gender is *always* determined by—er—sex," Mr. Parkhill hastily added. "We say 'she' for a country, for example, or a ship. But for newspapers one must use the neuter pronoun: 'it.' "

Mr. Kaplan thrashed in the coils of analysis. "Not masculine . . . not faminine . . . in de middle!"

Mr. Parkhill waited.

"Mr. Pockheel, I undistand abot masculine, faminine, an' neutral—"

" 'Neu*ter.* ' "

"—but shouldn't we say 'he' abot *som* papers? I mean, when a paper has a masculine *name?*"

Mr. Parkhill frowned. "I don't see what the name of a

134

paper has to do with it. When quoting *The New York Times,* for instance, we say 'It said.' Or of the *New York Post,* we say 'It said.' Or—"

"*Dose* papers," Mr. Kaplan conceded benignly. "But when a paper has a real masculine name?"

"And which paper," asked Mr. Parkhill, slightly amused, "would you say has a truly—'masculine' name?"

Mr. Kaplan's features dripped modesty. "Harold Tribune."

(P.S. To the young and the British: The *New York Herald Tribune,* a most distinguished daily, expired in 1962.)

11

MR. K·A·P·L·A·N
CURES A HEADACHE

There were many evenings in the beginners' grade which Mr. Parkhill remembered with special clarity: the night Mr. Kaplan had delivered his surprising memorial to Jake Popper; the night Mr. Kaplan had reconstructed, in astonishing detail, the death of Julius Caesar. . . . Come to think of it, Mr. Parkhill reflected, most of the evenings he remembered—surely those he remembered most vividly— involved one or another of Mr. Kaplan's mind-boggling alterations of the English language.

He idly wondered, this pleasant night, when both windows of the schoolroom were wide open and a sweet breeze freshened the air, what conceivable feats of innovation, what monstrous flights of false logic, Mr. Kaplan could possibly extract from the simple homework assignment for this evening: a one-page composition, on any topic, which six students had already transcribed on (and five had read aloud from) the blackboard.

Mr. C. J. Fledermann had fashioned a commendable description of "Castles in the Rhine." Mr. Milas Wodjik had written a crisp letter to his twin brother, Tomas, who, standing at the board right next to him, had written a crisp letter to Milas.

Miss Lola Lopez had produced a rather fervent vignette on the noble character and historic achievements of *"El*

Libertador," Simón Bolivar, who had fought Spanish tyranny in such lands as Colombia, Venezuela, Peru—in none of which Miss Lopez, who came from Havana, confessed she ever had the good fortune to reside.

Mr. Nathan P. Nathan had speedily transcribed his homework (he had actually written it in the classroom, before the opening bell) with a running obbligato of private laughs. The composition was an account of the breathless last moments of a basketball game against Mr. Nathan's team's arch-rival, Ashkenazi's Aces:

> Score 72–72. The croud yells crazy. Dopey Dave got the ball. He passes to me. Nosey Prishkin is garding me and trys a steall. *He fowls!* Croud is more crazy. I go to line. Boy was I nervus! But I breat deep, take my time, and sink the ball in. Boy! Game is dun. So we win 73–72.
>
> I sure am proud of my teem.

Mr. Nathan had made remarkable progress in the months during which, at intervals, he had attended the A.N.P.S.A. If only he would subject his spelling to a portion of the discipline he expended on his foul shots, Mr. Parkhill sighed. . . .

Now, only the homework of Miss Mitnick awaited class autopsy. She had placed her composition on the board in a hand as dainty and diminutive as her personality. Blushing, stammering, she read the sentences aloud:

My Work—a Waitress

My job is as waitress in a cafeteria. It has the name "Meckler's 4-Star Famous." I am working 9 hours a day, from 7–½ in morning to 4–½ after-noon.

We are serving breakfast, lunch (also luncheons, they are smaller) and supper—or "dinner" like Americans say. But I go home before.

My work is to stand behind counter. Giving Coffee, Tea, Ice Tea, or cold Milk—as customers ask. It is not so hard.

But I get tired from standing all day. And sometime I have
bad headackes.

My pay is not too good, but I am happy for having *any* job.
People should be happy for having work. Because all over
the world is hard times.

Thank you.

Miss Mitnick stopped. The blush had left her cheeks; she
was as pale as an oyster.

"Dandy, Rose, just *dan*dy!" laughed Mr. Nathan.

"That *is* good," said Mr. Parkhill. "There are some mistakes, naturally—in punctuation, in the use of prepositions; but on the whole, Miss Mitnick, that is *ex*cellent!"

Giddied by such praises, Rose Mitnick reeled to the sanc-
tuary of her seat.

"Now then, corrections." Mr. Parkhill smiled. "Please
study Miss Mitnick's work carefully, class. Jot down any
mistakes you see. In a few minutes, I shall call for volunteers."

The scholars slid into the sea of concentration, their
brows a wave of furrows, their lips tightened bulkheads of
resolution. Reuben Olansky (after walking up to the blackboard to examine the words, his nose almost scraping the
slate) scribbled corrections on an envelope. Rochelle Goldberg chewed a Tootsie Roll to fortify her faculties. Mr.
Blattberg strengthened his cerebration by fingering the
watch chain from which his heirs' incisors gleamed. And
Hyman Kaplan, who had been unusually sedate throughout the evening ("I can't corract about besketball because
I never even saw one in poisson!"), shot one penetrating
glance at Miss Mitnick's essay, uttered a premonitory
"Aha!" and proceeded to ply his pen across his trusty journal.

Mr. Parkhill sauntered down the aisle. "I'll give the class
a hint," he said lightly. "There's one word—only one in the
entire composition, I may say to Miss Mitnick's credit—
that is *spelled* wrong."

The class glanced from the board to their paragon, who turned crimson. But Mr. Kaplan did not look up; he was scribbling away in a fever.

"You need not spend too much time—er—*elaborating* on Miss Mitnick's mistakes," said Mr. Parkhill uneasily. "Just make brief notes. That will give you more time to examine punctuation . . . prepositions. . . ." (Prepositions were the Achilles' heel of the beginners' grade.)

Mr. Parkhill strolled back, up the aisle. Mr. Pinsky's squint suggested that he had spotted several flagrant errors. Miss Atrakian was crooning Armenian affirmations over her tablet. Mr. Trabish tossed between yawning and exegesis. And Mr. Kaplan, lost in some holy mission, was breathing heavily.

"Very well, class. Who will be the first volunteer? Corrections?"

To his surprise, Mrs. Moskowitz raised a pudgy palm. "Shouldn't be in Miss Mitnick's assay 'l' on the end of 'cafeteria'?"

"I'm—afraid not," said Mr. Parkhill. (Mrs. Moskowitz had the unfortunate habit of adding an "l" to nearly all nouns ending in a vowel; she once purchased a "neck tiel" for her husband, had changed the covers on her "sofal," and always asked the grocer to give her fresh "tomatols.")

"More comments?"

"Not enough definite articles!" declaimed Isaac Nussbaum. "It should be '*a* waitress,' '*the* morning,' '*the* counter'—and even 'before' *something!* You can't just be 'before'!" Mr. Nussbaum certainly was in top form tonight.

"Very good," said Mr. Parkhill, adding four articles to Miss Mitnick's offering. "We might all pay closer attention to our definite—and indefinite—articles. . . . Mr. Trabish?"

"People should be happy *to* work," announced Mr. Trabish, "not '*for*' work—"

"Correct."

"—although *I* am myself heppy for *and* to."

Approval danced across the ranks: no one had suspected baker Trabish, who sometimes slept through an entire evening, of possessing such keen perception.

"Miss Kipnis?"

"In my poisonal opinion," opined Miss Kipnis, *"lunch* is what men are eating, but *luncheons,* which Miss Mitnick says are smaller, is what ladies eat."

"Well . . ." Mr. Parkhill tactfully suggested that some men, when in a hurry, often ate luncheons, too. "In fact, some restaurants feature a 'Business Man's Luncheon.' "

"That's nice," said "Cookie" Kipnis.

"Who will be next?"

The congregation was silent.

"Come, come. There are several more mistakes . . . Mr. Kaplan?"

"Is *planty* mistakes by Mitnick, but"—Mr. Kaplan paused sententiously—"I am not raddy."

Mr. Parkhill looked puzzled. "Er—why not just give us the mistakes you have already discovered?" He nodded toward Mr. Kaplan's notebook.

"I'm only beginnink." Mr. Kaplan held up his Doomsday book. What had taken so much of Mr. Kaplan's effort was a printed legend:

> ### Mistakes by Mitnick
> (on Black-board)
> *by*
> H*Y*M*A*N K*A*P*L*A*N

The rest of the page was blank.

At least, Mr. Parkhill consoled himself, Mr. Kaplan had learned how to spell "blackboard"; heretofore he had deformed it into "blackbored," "bleckbort," and even "blackbroad."

Mrs. Pilpul raised an imperious ruler. "It should not be by Miss Mitnick a *number* 'one-half' after the 'seven,' and also after the 'four.' That way is for *sizes*—like in stockings, or two-and-half pounds meat, or happles."

"That's a very good point," said Mr. Parkhill.

"'*Vun*-half' is for socks, not clocks," declared Mr. Kaplan.

Mr. Pinsky slapped his thigh in appreciation of this *bon mot.*

"Class, how should 'half-past seven' and 'half-past four' be written?"

For a moment it appeared that no one in the beginners' grade knew how half-past seven and half-past four should be rendered. Then Christian Fledermann said, "Wiz *numbers:* a seven-sree-zero and a four-sree-zero!"

"Excellent!" Mr. Parkhill erased "7-½" and "4-½" and, on a playful inspiration, wrote "730" and "430." "Like *this,* Mr. Fledermann?" He raised an eyebrow.

Mr. Kaplan had learned that whenever Mr. Parkhill raised an eyebrow, the answer was "No." "No!" he sang out.

"I was addressing Mr. Fledermann," said Mr. Parkhill coolly.

"*He* didn't enswer," said Mr. Kaplan.

"Perhaps you didn't give him time," said Mr. Parkhill icily. "Mr. Fledermann, are these correct?" Mr. Parkhill's pointer touched "730" and "430."

"N-no," said Mr. Fledermann warily.

"Dat's what *I* obsoived," said Mr. Kaplan.

Mr. Parkhill ignored him. "Like this, Mr. Fledermann?" He wrote "7–30" and "4–30." Again his eyebrows arched, so again Mr. Kaplan cried, "Dat looks like crecked dishes!"

Mr. Nathan shook with gratitude for so vivid a wit.

"Mr. Fledermann," scowled Mr. Parkhill.

"It ztill—don't *look* good," ventured Christian Fledermann.

"Of course not! Like *this?*" Mr. Parkhill made it "7/30"

and "4/30," one eyebrow arching gaily.

"Wrong!" blared Mr. Kaplan. "Mish-mosh!"

"This mon is crazy," moaned Olga Tarnova. "He has *balyéza!*"

"Soon *he'll* be the titcher!" glowered Reuben Olansky.

"Well, class," said Mr. Parkhill unhappily, "Mr. Kaplan happens to be right. . . . *All* of these signs are wrong for the representation of time." Impressed by Mr. Kaplan's rapid negations, Mr. Parkhill asked, "Can you tell the class the correct form?"

Mr. Kaplan's smile congealed. "De *corract* form?"

"Yes."

"We did not have dis subject in cless."

Mr. Parkhill blinked. "We *did,* some time ago. But—do you know?"

"What?"

"Which mark of punctuation to use when indicating *time."*

"Not yat," finessed Mr. Kaplan.

Unfriendly snorts and sneers countered Mr. Kaplan's canny subterfuge.

"Some chip trick!" bawled Mr. Blattberg.

"Hoo-hoo!" hooted Mr. Hruska.

"Mr. Kaplen *edmits* he don't know something?" gaped Mrs. Shimmelfarb.

"He didn't edmit!" cried loyal Pinsky. "He avoided!"

"Oy!" smiled Mrs. Moskowitz, no easy feat.

"I'll bust!" laughed Nathan P. Nathan.

"Class . . . order. . . ." Mr. Parkhill felt let down by Mr. Kaplan. Not because Mr. Kaplan had canceled the achievement of knowing what was wrong by not knowing what was right: that was a common failing. What disappointed Mr. Parkhill was that Mr. Kaplan had been so cocksure in his rejections of the hyphen and the slash that he had lured Mr. Parkhill into assuming that he did know

the correct answer. . . . Mr. Parkhill inserted colons after "7" and "4." He touched the "7:30" and the "4:30" with his pointer. "How about *this* way, class?"

"Poifick!" cracked Mr. Kaplan, for Mr. Parkhill's eyebrows had remained inert.

"Mr. Kaplan is right." Mr. Parkhill was both impressed and mystified. "This mark, class, is used to indicate time, and in many other ways—to introduce a list, say, or a quotation, or after the salutation, 'Dear Sir' or 'Dear Madam' in a letter." On a portion of the blackboard he made clean with the eraser, Mr. Parkhill chalked two large dots, one below the other, in a magnified colon. "What do we call this mark, class?"

Hemmings and hawings betrayed their ignorance.

"Anyone?"

No one.

"It's a very *useful* mark of punctuation, class. . . ."

"I wish I knew it!" grinned Mr. Nathan. "Rose, tell the teacher. *Guess,* even."

Miss Mitnick said timidly, "Semicolon?"

"Not *quite.* But you are close, Miss Mitnick! *Very* close. This is not a 'semicolon' but a—"

Up shot one pen of Hyman Kaplan.

"Mr. Kaplan."

"Two periods!"

A pang pierced Mr. Parkhill's spine. *"No,* Mr. Kaplan! That was a most *un*fortunate guess. This is called a *colon."* He quickly returned to Miss Mitnick's essay, concealing his dismay, changing a tense here, a dependent clause there, making every correction, indeed, except one: Miss Mitnick's glaring "headackes." He faced his students. "I have left just one mistake in Miss Mitnick's work—the mistake in spelling I mentioned earlier. Who can find it?"

Once more, his flock mobilized their energies. Miss Mitnick stared intently at her sentences, yearning to expunge

143

her disgrace by being first to remedy her blunder. The widow Pilpul scrutinized the board without mercy. Mr. Olansky donned a fiercer expression, as if to intimidate the distant prose. Nathan P. Nathan, knowing the boundaries of his knowledge, simply laughed. And Mr. Kaplan, invigorating his critical powers through incantation, murmured each word aloud: "My—job—is—as—waitress. . . . Aha! In 'waitress' should be no 'i'!"

"No, Mr. Kaplan. 'Waitress' comes from 'wait,' and 'wait' contains an 'i.' "

Mr. Kaplan looked wounded.

Mr. Umea rejoiced.

Miss Mitnick stammered, "I think m-my 'headaches' is spelled wrong."

"Ufcawss!" cried Mr. Kaplan. " 'Hadakes' is spalled wrong!"

"That is what Miss Mitnick said." Mr. Parkhill could not resist the deserved rebuke, nor an ironic invitation: "Perhaps you will favor us by spelling it right."

" 'Had-akes' is two woids in vun. . . ."

"Yes, Mr. Kaplan. So we spell it just as if we were spelling the two separate 'words'—not 'woids.' If you simply combine 'head' and 'aches'. . . ." Mr. Parkhill lifted the chalk to the board. "Would you spell—?"

Mr. Kaplan misconstrued the invitation and leaped to the blackboard, where, as friend and foe alike held their breath, he printed:

H-E-A-D-A-X-E

For a horrified moment, Mr. Parkhill was struck silent, as silent as his scholars, who were uncertain whether Mr. Kaplan had committed a new crime or made a contribution to orthography. At last, Mr. Parkhill shook his head, erased the gruesome HEADAXE and wrote HEADACHES in its place. Once more had Hyman Kaplan massacred an expectation he had so clearly, so recklessly, aroused.

12

DAYMARE AT WATERLOO

American Rev. Goodby England. U.S. solders died.
Civil war. Salves no more barefoot.
Solders died in North. Solders died in South.
World War. Making world save for Democracy. Solders
died. Sailors died.
World War again. Solders, sailors, plain pilots died.
These are for why now we put on their graves flowers,
same as anyone, May 30. This is my virgin of Memo. Day.

—Mary Atrakian

Mr. Parkhill leaned back in his easy chair. Two nights
ago, he had given his students a little lecture on Memorial
Day, how Arlington Cemetery is its focus and the Unknown Soldier its shrine. He had been careful to point out
that every land honors those fallen in battle. He had
shown the class pictures of the Cenotaph in London, the
Arc de Triomphe, Red Square (at which point Olga Tarnova, a progeny of White Russia, had hissed with fervor).

Now, correcting the homework in the easy chair in his
lodgings, Mr. Parkhill realized that his words and pictures
had made a deeper impression than he had anticipated.
He started to correct Miss Atrakian's eulogy, feeling re-
lieved that she had written, rather than spoken, her heart-
felt words. There would have been no problem in his ex-
plaining the word "version" to the class; but "virgin"—!

145

"Virgin," Mr. Parkhill could not help thinking, bristled with all sorts of dangers, given the volatile types in the beginners' grade.

He turned to the next paper. It was by Fanny Gidwitz. On the first page was printed only this title:

SOLDEIRS AND SAILORS—HURRY!

Mr. Parkhill read this three times before meaning came. His red pencil raced across the page:

Miss G—
    You mean "Hurrah!"—or "Hooray!" There is all the difference in the world between "Hurray" (or "Hooray") and "hurry."

                             —Mr. P.

He was frankly disappointed in Miss Gidwitz.

He turned to the next paper. To his surprise (now that he thought of it, the compositions had been chock-full of surprises), a poem met his eyes:

I

Today remember
Last December
Was no place
For Decoration Days

II

Soldeirs, sailors,
Airplaners, Marines
Shouldn't stand only
By hot-dog machines
    —Nathan P. Nathan

Who would have dreamed that beneath the frivolous façade of Mr. Nathan flowed such lyrical emotions?

He corrected the spelling of "soldiers," wrote " 'Pilots,' not 'airplaners,' " and added "Good effort, Mr. N!" (He did not think it wise to comment on the incongruity of "hot-dog machines.")

The next opus, a letter from Mr. Christian J. Fleder-mann to someone addressed as "Deer Heinrich," contained this thought:

> In old times, armies moved very slow, but today everything goes quack-quack.

At that moment, Mr. Parkhill decided it was time to drill the class vigorously once more on antonyms. One of the most useful byproducts of homework was that it gave Mr. Parkhill time away from the pressures of the classroom (the clash of egos, the partisan storms) to think up lessons specifically designed to remedy specific, persistent errors. "Antonyms!" he thought, as he doffed his slippers. "They are *pretty* shaky on their antonyms."

He opened the very next session of the class by announcing, "Tonight, class, we shall concentrate on our Opposites." (He would not dream of inflicting "antonyms" on his fledglings.) "Notebooks, please. Write five nouns in one column, and write their opposites—opposite." The play on words pleased him. (He could never understand why Miss Higby, according to all reports, conducted her class with such humorless rigor.) "We shall then place our lists on the blackboard for group comment."

It was heartening to see how the students welcomed the assignment. Opposites seemed to enlist their enthusiasm —unlike indirect objects, which they resented, or irregular verbs, which they loathed. Opposites were honest, open, above-board. Confidence bloomed in the forum.

Mr. C. J. Fledermann unbuttoned his vest and sharpened his pencil cheerfully. Miss Ziev set pen to paper with zest. (The banns for Miss Ziev's marriage to Mr. Andrassy had officially been posted.) Mr. Trabish even reversed a yawn in midstream, transforming torpidity to approval by a mere rerouting of breath. And Mr. Kaplan, that visionary gleam in his eye, cried, "Opposites! My!"

It promised to be a fruitful evening. Mr. Parkhill strolled down the aisle, nodding and smiling; his apprentices smiled and clucked in return. When he reached the back of the room, he raised a window. He noticed that some light bulbs in the electric sign at the end of the street, "Tip Top Used Cars," faintly flickered: the sign sometimes read "Tip Top Used Curs." (Mr. Studniczka might have written that. Poor Peter Ignatius Studniczka. He had been plunged into such despair by the past perfect tense that he had surrendered to defeat, and had never returned to the school. . . .)

Mr. Parkhill ambled back, up the aisle, glancing with interest at notebooks in which opposites were sprouting like mushrooms.

After several minutes, Mr. Parkhill announced, "One minute more . . ." and in two minutes called, "Time. . . . Are we ready? . . . Good! Will the following please go to the board? Miss Mitnick . . . Mr. Nussbaum . . . Mrs. Shimmelfarb . . ." He called six names in all.

It was a buoyant platoon that advanced upon the blackboard, and a triumphant one that returned. Their chalked columns were a tribute to Mr. Parkhill's tutelage. Not a single mistake marred the quintet of antonyms Miss Mitnick had provided:

Silence	Noise
Gloomy	Happy
Weak	Strong
Fancy	Plain
Smart	Stupid

Only one tiny lapse in spelling blemished Mr. Nussbaum's counterparts: "Fresh . . . stole." Miss Kipnis had produced four excellent antonyms, tripping only on the opposite of "wet," which she rendered as "fry," and Mrs. Yanoff harbored the understandable illusion that the op-

148

posite of "freedom" is "jail." But all things considered, antonyms had gotten off to a flying start.

Soon Mr. Parkhill sent six more scholars to the board. None turned in as faultless a performance as Miss Mitnick's, but none committed a gaffe as queer as Mr. Nussbaum's either. . . .

Another sextet was dispatched to the board. Mr. Parkhill felt quite cheerful, even optimistic. Nothing so warms the cockles of a teacher's heart as progress—visible, unmistakable progress—in his flock.

He smiled at the board. From her tiptoed stance, Lola Lopez had neatly written, in tiny letters that seemed fitting for so petite a form:

baby	boy
child	man
man	woman
save	spend
hello	solong

Reuben Olansky was printing, in the mammoth hand of the myopic:

sick	normal
over	under
front	back
death	life
strong	wick

At once Mr. Parkhill saw how he would approach the correcting of "wick."

He turned to Mr. Hruska's offering. Learning came hard to Mr. Hruska. Scowling, perspiring, muttering discontents, Vasil Hruska had but partly scaled the battlements of English:

black	white
white	black

149

Mr. Parkhill sighed. It was a long, hard row Vasil Hruska had to hoe—but hoe it, Mr. Parkhill had no doubt, he would.

The next pupil at the board was Mr. Kaplan. Mr. Parkhill braced himself. And after but one glance at what Hyman Kaplan had this time conjured out of the carnival of his mind, Mr. Parkhill turned his back to the board. *Frangas, non flectes:* the man might break, but he would never bend.

What *could* one do about Mr. Kaplan? It was discouraging to confront such impediments—novel, even ingenious, but still impediments—to instruction.

Mr. Kaplan was standing before the board in bliss, hand on hip, eyes enraptured, a Robert La Salle on the bank of the Ohio; and Mr. Parkhill, even from the back of the chamber, could hear La Salle humming—humming just loud enough for everyone in the room to share his ecstasy.

What induced such beatitude in Mr. Kaplan's soul was (1) performing at the blackboard, which he loved; (2) envisaging the broil and brabble of discussion, which he adored; (3) contemplating the wonders of the human brain, of which his was so scintillating a model:

H*Y*M*A*N K*A*P*L*A*N
gives
5 Opp.

The name, as always, gleamed like a banner: the bright stars relieving the loneliness between one letter and another. It grieved Mr. Kaplan that Mr. Parkhill had made him desist from using colors on the slate to outline the letters and illuminate the stars; and, in truth, the deprivation made the name anemic. Under his triumphant title, the Ariel of the beginners' grade had written:

Can Man live without Opp? No! Why? Without opp. is impossible to discuss anything.

Soppose someone hollers, "Wrong!" How can you say "Right"? Only with an opp.!

So Mr. Parkhill gives a fine lesson—5 opp.

So Hyman Kaplan is happy to presant:

Word	Opp.
1. Spic	span
2. Tall	shrimp
3. N. Dakota	S. Dakota

Mr. Kaplan was searching the ledges for a fresh stick of chalk.

Mr. Parkhill wiped his brow. It was not going to be an easy evening, after all.

"Take your seats, please." Mr. Parkhill glanced at the clock. "Miss Lopez . . ."

Miss Lopez read her words as if they were caged birds, and her opposites as if releasing them from captivity.

"Any corrections?" asked Mr. Parkhill.

"Not vun!" cried Mr. Kaplan promptly. "Congradulation, Lipschitz!" (Why Mr. Kaplan converted "Lopez" to "Lipschitz" only God could explain.)

"The opposite of 'hello' is really 'good-bye,' " Mr. Parkhill told Miss Lopez. "Mr. Olansky."

Reuben Olansky put his notebook to within an inch of his nose to read his words (he could never make out the glyphs on a distant blackboard): "Sick . . . normal. Front . . . back. Strong . . . wick."

"Mistake!" called Miss Mitnick.

"Yes?" (Mr. Parkhill could always rely on Rose Mitnick.)

"The opposite of 'strong' is spelled wrong."

"How *should* it be spelled?"

"W-e-a-k," said Miss Mitnick.

"Exactly!" Mr. Parkhill smiled; Mr. Kaplan's face fell.

" 'Weak,' Mr. Olansky, is not *'wick.'* " He wrote WEAK and WICK on the crowded slate. "You see, class, why we must be so careful in pronunciation? The short 'i' is *not* the long 'e' and—uh—vice versa. That is what is at the root of Mr. Olansky's difficulty. . . . Now, who can tell us what 'w*i*ck' means?"

Before anyone could so much as make a stab at what "w-i-c-k" meant, Mr. Kaplan sang out, "Point of order!"

Mr. Parkhill frowned. He was not accustomed to hearing protocol invoked in the beginners' grade. "Y-yes?"

"Didn't you jost say de void *'vick'* is wrong?" inquired Mr. Kaplan.

"I said that 'w*i*ck' is not 'w*ea*k.' "

"So 'wick' isn't wrong!" Mr. Olansky jeered righteously. "Just different."

"Well," Mr. Parkhill said unhappily, " 'wick' is wrong as the *opposite* of—"

"Wrong *an'* different?!" cried Mr. Kaplan. "So Olansky made two mistakes instad of vun!"

"Mr. Kap—"

"But 'wick' is a real word!" protested Reuben Olansky.

"So is 'pastrami'!" observed Mr. Kaplan. "But it's not de opposite of 'ice cream'!"

Mr. Olansky fell into piteous yammerings. Mr. Nathan howled.

"Mr. Kaplan!" Mr. Parkhill tapped his chalk on the desk sternly. "We can dispense with—sarcasm. Let us return to the question I asked. Who can tell us the meaning of 'wick'?"

Earnest brows furrowed as earnest eyes focused on "wick": sixty lips tightened as thirty minds probed for "wick" 's innermost secret.

"It's quite a—*common* word," said Mr. Parkhill hopefully.

Up sailed the palm of Hyman Kaplan.

Mr. Parkhill pretended not to see it. *"Anyone?"* he asked.

No one responded to "Anyone?" save Mr. Kaplan, who began to swing his arm like a reversed pendulum.

Mr. Parkhill wrestled with his conscience, and finally sighed, "Very well. . . ."

"Savan days make vun wick!" declaimed Mr. Kaplan.

"No, no, no!" Mr. Parkhill winced. "That is a 'week'!" He was quite cross with Mr. Kaplan, and so reproachful in applying the chalk that it broke. With a fresh stick he wrote:

WEEK
WEAK
WICK

"My!" exclaimed Mr. Kaplan. "I fond a toid woid!"

" 'Week,' " said Mr. Parkhill, "means seven days. But 'weak' "—he tapped the second word with his pointer—"means not strong. And 'wick' "—he tapped the third word sharply—"is the cord or thread inside a candle, the part that burns!"

A chorale ascended from the enlightened.

"Oooh!"

"I see!"

"Haddaya like that?!"

It was ever thus: the revelation of a new word was like the establishment of another beachhead on the spiky shores of English.

"Like in a cigarette lighter, I have a wick!" exclaimed Olaf Umea.

"Wick, weak, *week*," practiced Isaac Nussbaum.

"W*ea*k . . . week . . . w*i*ck," intoned Olga Tarnova, a weary whippoorwill.

Mr. Parkhill next called upon Vasil Hruska.

Mr. Hruska clutched his necktie. " 'Black . . . white. White . . . black. One . . . two. Two . . . one. Eat . . . not eat.' . . . I hope." His shoulders sagged.

Before Mr. Parkhill could offer a therapeutic word, Mr. Olansky, smarting under his wounds, lashed out, "What kind of opposite is 'not eat'?"

"Emoigency kind!" retorted Mr. Kaplan, who would defend anyone Mr. Olansky attacked. "You axpact a hongry man to use poifick gremmer?"

"Who said anything about diet?" yowled Mr. Olansky.

Mr. Kaplan averted his eyes piously.

"But 'not eat,' " stammered Miss Mitnick, "isn't an opposite."

"Why not?"

"Because—"

"Ha! 'Because' isn't a rizzon; it's a conjonction!" Before this unexpected feat of grammar from Mr. Kaplan, Miss Mitnick flinched.

"*Mr.* Kaplan!" Mr. Parkhill made no attempt to conceal his displeasure. "Mr. Olansky and Miss Mitnick are quite right. 'Not eat' is *not* an opposite. It is, I'm sorry to say, not a good phrase in any sense." He erased "not eat" with one firm swipe of the eraser. "Mr. Olansky, what is the opposite of 'eat'?"

Mr. Olansky blinked blankly. "Eh . . . ah . . . kh . . ."

"Ai-ai-ai," crooned Mr. Kaplan. "Hruska at least didn't sond like he's gargling!"

Furious, Mr. Olansky searched for Mr. Kaplan through the wrong half of his bifocals. "Maybe *you* know the opposite of 'eat'?"

"I," said Mr. Kaplan with dignity, "vasn't called on by Mr. Pockheel!"

"Stop!" roared Mr. Olansky. "You wiggle-piggle out of every—"

"The opposite of 'eat,' " announced Mr. Parkhill loudly, "may be one of several words. . . ." He wrote FAST and STARVE on the board. (He wished he could reprimand Hyman Kap—but one can hardly tell a full-grown man to stand in the corner.) "And Mr. Hruska, since 'black' is the opposite of 'white,' then 'white' is obviously the opposite of 'black.' And 'one' and 'two' are *numbers,* not opposites. Can you think of any other words?"

Mr. Hruska pondered dolefully. His face reddened, but his cerebration froze.

"Just look around the *room,"* suggested Mr. Parkhill. "You will see many—opposites." He lifted his eyes to the ceiling, then lowered his head to the floor. He touched his head, then lifted his foot. He touched his chest, then turned his back. (Would Plaut and Biberman—Professor Samish had drowned, most unexpectedly, a year ago, and Dr. Luther Biberman had co-authored the new, sparkling edition of *Teaching English to Foreigners*—approve?)

Mr. Hruska had been following every move of Mr. Parkhill's pantomime in fascination.

"Now, can you think of a pair of opposites?" asked Mr. Parkhill.

"Yos! 'Butter . . . bread'!"

How on earth Mr. Hruska associated ceiling-floor, head-foot, chest-back, with butter and bread, Mr. Parkhill could not imagine.

"Mr. Hruska, 'butter' and 'bread' certainly *go* together, but I think it is stretching the point a bit to—er—call them opposites. . . ."

Mr. Parkhill glanced at the clock. He hoped that no time remained, for Mr. Kaplan's opposites were next. But the hands of the clock overlapped at 10 minutes to 10, and Mr. Kaplan was already rising and smiling. "Mr. Kaplan," Mr. Parkhill quickly said, "before I call upon you, *may* I remind you that the assignment calls only for five words and five opposites? We—er—do not want a speech, nor a lengthy introduction!"

How often had Mr. Parkhill tried to restrain Mr. Kaplan, who approached the most routine assignment as if it might lead to the Legion of Honor? Mr. Parkhill had never been able to check that exuberant imagination. It was like asking a gladiator to strike only one blow, or Magellan to cross only one sea.

Already a few students, scouting Mr. Kaplan's work in anticipation with that hawklike zeal they reserved for the weasel in their midst, were chortling. A cocksure sneer sped from Mr. Olansky to Mr. Barbella (it was intended for Mr. Blattberg beside him); a knowing gloat winged from Mrs. Yanoff to Mrs. Pilpul. Miss Tarnova plied an inscrutable smile along her inscrutable lips and honed her handkerchiefed dagger for the carnage to come.

For once, Mr. Kaplan did not respond to criticism as if it were decapitation. He was too busy alerting his small band of acolytes. "Trabish! Wake op!"

"Just read your words from your chair!" Mr. Parkhill ordered.

Mr. Kaplan flinched. "Not go to the bort?"

"You can see the words quite clearly from your chair! And that's all you need read: the *words!*"

Mr. Kaplan lamented man's inhumanity to man, summoned support from the arsenals of faith, and read bravely: " 'Fife opposites by Hyman Keplen'!" (The title, apparently, could be smuggled into the category of "words.") " 'Spic . . . span,' " recited the hobbled bard. " 'Tall . . . shrimp.' 'Naut Dakota . . . Sot Dakota.' 'Talk . . . sharop.' 'Nightmare . . . daymare.' "

Mr. Parkhill wheeled toward the board in astonishment. There it was, all right, in Mr. Kaplan's unmistakable script: "Nightmare ***** daymare."

"Hanh?!" cried Mr. Blattberg.

A malediction came from Miss Tarnova.

"Pssh!" Mr. Pinsky slapped his cheek in admiration.

Miss Mitnick's mouth was a circle of horror. Mr. Nathan was doubled over.

Mr. Parkhill debated how to proceed. "Nightmare . . . daymare."

Fists, fingers, pencils, rulers were waving wildly, supplemented by pleas and petitions: "Mr. Parkhill!" "Titcher!" "Mistake! Mistake!"

"Class . . ." he said in a bit of a daze. "You may lower your hands and—er—other objects. Everyone will have a turn. . . . We shall take up Mr. Kaplan's mistakes one at a time."

Mr. Kaplan's jaw dropped. Not "Mr. Kaplan's mistake" but "Mr. Kaplan's *mistakes.*" And "Everyone will have a turn. . . ." And "one at a time. . . ." Mr. Kaplan started a deep-breathing exercise.

"Mr.—Fledermann," called Mr. Parkhill.

C. J. Fledermann declared pettishly that since "spic" was not the opposite of "span," "span" could not masquerade as the opposite of "spic." " 'Spic *and* span' can't be broken op!"

This *caveat* inspired Lucca Barbella to cry: "There isa no 'spica' by himself and no 'spana' also!"

"It's one *phrase,*" announced Miss Atrakian. "Like twins from Siam!"

This pleased the brothers Wodjik.

"*Cats* also come fromm Siam," purred Mr. Kaplan.

The *non sequitur* went unheeded.

So felicitous was the phrasing of Miss Atrakian, so vivid her imagery, that the entire Olansky-Blattberg-Nussbaum phalanx burst into applause. Miss Mitnick mustered up enough courage to titter.

The exultation scarcely thinned before Stanislaus Wilkomirski thundered that "shrimp" could not, by the most generous canons of usage, be accepted as the opposite of "tall." A shrimp, Mr. Wilkomirski shouted, was a fish, and no fish could be an opposite—"even a shark like Mr. Kaplan!"

Horselaughs certified the brilliance of the simile, and

guffaws vented the sweetness of revenge from those who had long suffered at Mr. Kaplan's hands.

Now Olga Tarnova—feline and mysterious—crooned, "Is not true thot to aducated people, North Dakota and South Dakota—both spelled wrong!—are *names*? So how can be one an opposite other? Can Pinsk be opposite of Minsk?" (Never had the milliner displayed such irony.) "Can Christmas be the opposite of New Year's? *Nyet!*"

"New York is opposite Brooklyn," flared Mr. Kaplan.

"Mr. Kaplan!" Mr. Parkhill was running out of patience. "Geography is not diction!"

"Good for Mr. Parkholl!" laughed Isaac Nussbaum.

"Kaplen, take asprin!" leered Olaf Umea.

Nathan P. Nathan covered his eyes and tossed about in his chair.

Miss Mitnick dropped her penguin air and entered the lists. "Nightmare . . . *day*mare?" Her cheeks were flushed. "I can't believe! Who ever heard such a word—such an *idea*—as a 'daymare'?"

The ranks rocked with new jubilation. Mr. Blattberg twirled his watch chain gleefully. Mr. Olansky bared his teeth in redemption. Miss Goldberg celebrated with halvah.

Mr. Parkhill was so busy replacing Mr. Kaplan's mistakes with antonyms fit for their duties that he did not notice what effect the merciless barrage was having upon its target. "Miss Mitnick is absolutely right, Mr. Kaplan! There is, strictly speaking, *no* opposite for 'nightmare.' I mean, when one does not have a nightmare, one simply has pleasant, untroubled sleep." He drew three implacable lines through "daymare," and asked, "Are you clear about all these corrections, Mr. Kaplan?"

Mr. Kaplan did not respond. He was gaping at his handiwork as if both he and it had been clubbed. So many corrections on what had seemed so spic-and-span a text. . . . So much ridicule, from such plebeian souls. . . . Mr.

Kaplan was horrified. He was mortified. He was crushed. There could be no doubt about it: Mr. Kaplan was at Waterloo. Defeat—massive and incontestable—had quashed Hyman Kaplan at last.

"Mr. Kaplan," Mr. Parkhill repeated, "is everything *clear?*"

Mr. Kaplan was as bereft of speech as he seemed to be of hearing.

Mr. Parkhill felt a twinge of remorse. Perhaps he should have spoken less sharply. Perhaps he should have stopped Mr. Kaplan's foes from slashing him to ribbons. He felt a pang of guilt, too: he *could* have intervened, and saved Mr. Kaplan's face. At the moment, that face looked ready for an embalmer.

The bell, for once merciful, chimed along the corridor.

At once, Mr. Parkhill called, "That will be all for tonight."

He had never seen the class so happy. They were chuckling and chortling—riding the rare rollers of revenge. Some students mouthed choice morsels from Mr. Kaplan's absurd antonyms; others bade him farewell—condescending or amused. Only Mr. Pinsky, fealty undimmed, glared defiance at those who had undone his prince.

"Koplon"—Miss Tarnova leaned over the prey like a presence out of Gogol—"you made enough mistakes tonight for whole year!"

"You learned a lesson?" mocked Mr. Blattberg.

"Next time don't confuse opposites and shmopposites!" Mr. Olansky resembled a malicious owl. "Agreed?"

Only then did some last, faint ember flicker in Hyman Kaplan's heart. "Agreet?" he echoed, all disdain, a man who might lose a battle but never a war. "No, Reuben Olansky. Naver, mine dear Tarnova. I'll give you all a prazant, a new opposite to remember: de opposite of 'agree.' . . . 'Nuts!' "

Mr. Parkhill felt as if he was having a daymare.

13

MR. K·A·P·L·A·N, EUMOIROUS
TO THE END

It had all begun so innocently, thought Mr. Parkhill. Only when the fume and foam of conflict had settled, many hours later and away from the seething scene of battle, could he organize his recollections.

Yet, how could he have known? Perhaps the time had something to do with it. The school year would soon be over; and when any semester approached its end, tempers grew tauter and patience wore thin. But where had things gone awry? With whose rash word? Whose brash quip? Which—

Perhaps it had started with the homework of Mr. Isaac Nussbaum, Orthodox cantor but unorthodox student, who had transcribed his composition on the blackboard: "Why Horses Die All Over." The opening was as electrifying as the title:

> Horses who have four legs are slower than autmobiles, and whose use makes horses die all over.

"Mr. Nussbaum," Mr. Parkhill had begun, "when you say 'horses who have four legs' (incidentally, we use 'who' for human beings, and 'which' or 'that' for animals) you imply that some horses do not have four legs."

Mr. Nathan burst into laughter. "Only fareaks!"

"Do you see my point, Mr. Nussbaum?"

"Yes, yes," the bearded one nodded. "How should it be changed?"

"Very simply," smiled Mr. Parkhill, "just—"

"Take the lags off the horses!" called Mr. Kaplan.

"Y-yes." Mr. Parkhill was pleased that Mr. Kaplan had improved so rapidly in recent months; that he was actually saying "the" instead of "de," and had even learned to use "off" instead of "from," which he had always pronounced "fromm." "I think the best thing to do is simply"—he drew a chalk line through "who have four legs"—"eliminate these four words! Now read the sentence."

" 'Horses are slower than—' Of course!" Mr. Nussbaum shook his head so happily that his skullcap slipped askew. "I don't *need* the 'who have four legs' at all!"

"Exactly." Mr. Parkhill then ran his pointer along the sentence, deliberately ignoring the misspelling of "automobiles," and stopped at the first word in the dependent clause: "and." That "and" was a perfect example of the superfluous conjunction, the grammatical fault Plaut and Biberman so aptly called "thwarted subordination."

Mr. Parkhill tapped the errant "and" three times. "You do not need this 'and' at all, either, Mr. Nussbaum. If we simply remove it"—Mr. Parkhill suited action to thought with one stroke of the eraser—"the proper relationship between the two ideas is preserved." He paused. "Automobiles do not 'make'—that is, *cause*—horses to die, Mr. Nussbaum. . . . Did you not mean to say that the automobile has *replaced* the horse?"

Mr. Nussbaum had no qualms about conceding that automobiles had replaced, rather than murdered, horses.

"Now, class, does anyone see a misspelled word in that sentence?"

" 'Automobile'!" That was reliable Miss Mitnick. "There should be an 'o' between 't' and 'm.' "

"Very good!" Mr. Parkhill inserted an "o" between the "t" and the "m."

And that, as he looked back upon it, was the fatal moment! Yes, that innocuous "o" was where the deplorable succession of events had begun. For "automobile" offered Mr. Parkhill a perfect opportunity to tell the class a bit about etymology—an exciting domain to students who knew languages other than English. Etymology could offer new and priceless clues to adults from abroad.

"Can anyone tell me *why* there should be an 'o' after the 't' in 'automobile'?" Mr. Parkhill smiled broadly.

Up went two fingers belonging to Hyman Kaplan.

"Yes?"

"There should be an 'o' efter 't' and before 'm' in 'automobile' because that's the way it's spelled!"

Mr. Parkhill did not try to disguise his disappointment. Circular reasoning had always been Mr. Kaplan's *forte,* and downfall. (But how Mr. Kaplan's pronunciation had improved! He had said "because" rather than "becawss," "spelled" instead of "spalled"; why, he was even saying "and" and "way" instead of "an'" and "vay" these days!)

"'Because that's the way it's spelled'?" Mr. Parkhill echoed. "*That* does not help a bit! That is simply—uh . . ."

"Because we need a vowel to squeeze in de sond 'o'?"

"N-no." With a stroke of the chalk, Mr. Parkhill separated "auto" from "mobile." He stepped back. "Notice, class: 'Automobile' consists of two parts—'auto' and 'mobile.' Now, the first part happens to come from Greek, the second from Latin. And each of these has a specific meaning. 'Mobile' means moving. 'Auto' is Greek for—"

"Yos! Yos!" Miss Atrakian was overjoyed. "'Auto' means—myself!"

"Exactly," said Mr. Parkhill. "So 'automobile' means 'self-moving,' moving under its own power, the 'auto' from Greek—"

"Now we stodying *Grik?*" cried Mrs. Moskowitz in horror. To Mrs. Moskowitz, the one thing English did not need was foreign aid—and enlargement—from yet another tongue.

"Did Greeks invent automobills?" blurted Vasil Hruska. "I thought it was Henry the Fourth."

"Henry 'For*d*'!"

"No!" Miss Atrakian snorted. " 'Automobile' is the word —Greek! 'Airplane' is Greek! 'Telephone' is Greek! All, all, all are Greek!"

Nationalism, which never lay more than a sliver beneath the simmering surface of the beginners' grade, bubbled through the room.

"Atrakian, don't be a hug! Leave a few screps for other nations!" charged Mr. Pinsky.

"Telephones came from Alexander Grayhound Bell," averred "Cookie" Kipnis.

"Airplanes are from U.S.," chirped Miss Lopez.

"Class . . . Miss Atrakian did not mean that the Greeks actually *invented* all these wonderful devices. She meant that the words which we use to *name* them are Greek—uh —in origin."

"Aahh . . ." drifted through the room.

"Oohhh," many murmured.

"Aha!" cried Hyman Kaplan, who scorned half measures.

Respectful glances showered upon Mary Atrakian, tendering her, as surrogate, the admiration her forebears richly deserved. (The fact that Miss Atrakian was Armenian, and bore as little love for Greeks as she did for Turks, was not known to her peers.)

Suddenly, the baritone of Lucca Barbella blasted the air. "Who giva da world Art?" he demanded. "Music? Paved roads? Roman arch? Galileo? Marconi? . . ." Mr. Barbella might have gone on cataloguing the genius of Rome had not even this brief sampling stung Olga Tarnova to the quick.

"Rossia! Rossia!" Miss Tarnova protested. "Tolstoy. Lermontov. Chakhov."

"Michelangelo! Leonardo! Rossini!" retorted Mr. Barbella.

"Ladies, gentlemen . . ." Mr. Parkhill was tapping his pointer on the desk. "We *must* dispense with such heated dialogue!"

"Also Greek!" cried C. J. Fledermann.

"Mr. *Parkhill* is Greek?" Mr. Wilkomirski, who was a riveter, could not trust his ears.

"'*Dialogue*' is Greek," snorted Mr. Fledermann, "not teacher."

"How come you know so much Greek and so little English?" laughed Nathan P. Nathan.

"He is a man of high culture!" snapped Mr. Olansky.

"Ha!" That was Kaplan. "Atrakian was *born* in Greece—"

"I was born in Bulgaria," protested Miss Atrakian.

"—so for dat she desoives a monument? T'ink, Olansky. Everybody got to loin *some* language. Greek is just her modder's tong."

"Her father spoke Grik, too!" retorted Mr. Umea.

Miss Atrakian had been trying (to no avail) to inform the class that her knowledge of Greek came from neither parent, but from her fiancé, whom she had met in Roseland, the mecca of ballroom dancing on Broadway.

"*Averyvun* in this room can talk a foreign tong!" Mr. Kaplan turned to Mr. Pinsky. "Pinsky, spik a few woids Rumanian."

"Mr. Kap—"

Mr. Pinsky uttered a few words in Rumanian.

"Wodjik!" Mr. Kaplan summoned a second underling. "Give a semple Polish."

Both Wodjiks, who were not Polish, promptly babbled

syllables from some indecipherable, but no doubt worthy, tongue.

"Nussbaum, say 'Hello and goodbye' in Hibrew!"

"No, no!" Mr. Parkhill drummed his pencil on the desk resolutely. "That will do, Mr. Kaplan." (He estimated that at least five other languages awaited Mr. Kaplan's summons.) "Let us return to the word 'automobile.' I was merely trying to point out that English is a living language. It is not fixed, unchanging. It grows all the time, adding new words, new shadings—"

"Oooo!" Poor Mrs. Moskowitz. To her, words were as immutable as mountains. To suggest that new words were being spawned right and left around her—that was opening the gates to bedlam.

"Let us take another word," said Mr. Parkhill quickly. He turned to the board and printed:

AUTOGRAPH

"Now, class, we saw that 'auto' refers to self. Does anyone know what 'graph' means?"

"Atrakian," Mr. Kaplan sighed, "you de only Grik in de cless."

"I—am—Armenian!"

"Close inoff."

Mr. Fledermann blurted, "I studied in Choiminy some Greek! So, 'Graph! . . . 'Grapho'! That means 'write'!"

"Very good, sir!" said Mr. Parkhill. "Therefore, 'autograph' means one's own handwriting, or signature. Now do you see, class?"

They not only saw; they were staggered.

"Wohnderful . . ." crooned Miss Tarnova.

"Haddaya like that?"

"Please, give more examples!"

"There are many, many more examples," said Mr. Parkhill gaily. He meditated for a moment. "Here is a word

165

which may strike you as—er—hard. I know it *looks* difficult—very difficult; yet I'm sure all of you have seen it dozens of times!" He printed:

HOMOGENIZED

Mr. Hruska fell off his chair.

"That's a *word?*" wailed "Cookie" Kipnis.

"What's a word?" asked Mr. Olansky, blinking with a ferocity that added nothing to his vision.

"Ooy," gasped Mrs. Moskowitz.

All around that intent forum, murmurs of uncertainty accompanied expressions of pain as the gruesome HOMOGENIZED defied their fathoming.

"Here is a hint to the ladies," said Mr. Parkhill. "Whenever you go into a food market, I am sure you see—" He rested his pointer on HOMOGENIZED.

"That?" sniffed Mrs. Yanoff. "Never."

"Who shops in a zoo?" asked the widow Pilpul.

"How can we buy something we can't pronounce?" asked Miss Goldberg.

Mr. Parkhill was not at all disheartened. "Now, now, ladies. *Think.* I can assure you that you have all seen this very word! Many times. . . . Does anyone have a clue?"

The blushing hand of Rose Mitnick rose. "Doesn't this mean a certain kind of milk?"

"It certainly does!" said Mr. Parkhill heartily.

"Good girl, Rose!" laughed Nathan P. Nathan.

"Meelk?!" gulped Lola Lopez.

"Goodness sek!" Miss Ziev scribbled a note that would enliven many a dinner after she was Mrs. Andrassy.

"I knew you would recognize it!" beamed Mr. Parkhill. "Now, 'homogenized' milk will take on a *much* richer meaning once we understand what its separate parts mean."

He raised his chalk and with one swift stroke bisected

HOMOGENIZED. " 'Homo' means 'like,' or 'the same.' 'Genos' refers to 'type' or 'kind.' Homogenized milk, therefore, is a milk which is the same throughout, milk in which the cream has been thoroughly distributed—"

"You mean I am drinking *Greek* milk?" Miss Atrakian was scandalized.

"No!"

"Greek milk is from goats!" smirked Olaf Umea.

"I am not a goat!"

"You are not a cow eider," said Mr. Kaplan, "but you drink American milk!"

At this point, Lucca Barbella, who was becoming increasingly hostile to Hellas, broke in to ask Mr. Parkhill whether Greek was the *only* language which had enriched the Anglo-Saxon. Had not a certain other noble tongue endowed English with rare linguistic treasures? Through both his question and his intonation, which suggested an overheated diplomat delivering an icy *démarche,* Mr. Barbella practically accused Mr. Parkhill of playing favorites among the nations.

"Latin," Mr. Parkhill promptly agreed, "has probably contributed even more words to English than Greek has."

"Bravo," said Mr. Barbella.

"We have to learn still *anodder* lengvidge?" quaked Mrs. Moskowitz.

"My nephew writes Latin," Mr. Wilkomirski announced.

"What?!"

"You teasing?!"

"He is doctor," said Mr. Wilkomirski.

"Class, suppose we now try a few words with Latin roots. It is extremely interesting!" Onto the board sprang:

POSTPONE

"Now, 'post' means 'after,' and 'pone' comes from 'ponere' —to 'place.' So 'postpone' means—"

167

"Tea!"

Mr. Parkhill stopped short. "I beg your pardon?"

"Tea!" It was Reuben Olansky.

" 'Tea'?" echoed Mr. Parkhill, somewhat bewildered. " 'Tea' is not a Latin—"

"It's Chinee!" boomed Mr. Olansky. "You asked for foreign words in—"

"Oh, I see what you mean. Yes, 'tea' is, I believe, from the Chinese—"

"Zwieback!"

Mr. Parkhill coughed. "What?"

"Zwieback!" Mr. C. J. Fledermann insisted. "From Cherman."

"Oh, yes!"

"Man alife!" exclaimed Mr. Kaplan. "Aren't any woids in English fromm *England?*"

"Englond? Bah!" Olga Tarnova flicked her handkerchief at Albion. "Englond is not romahnteek. Englond is football, sail-boys. *Whare is Englond's soul?* . . . Rossia! Rossia has most beautiful worrds. *Zvezda,* that means 'star.' *Syértse*—that is 'heart'! *Píshushchaya mashína*—'typewriter'!"

That was all that was needed to rouse those who carried the Mediterranean in their blood.

"Those wordsa are *Russian!*" snarled Mr. Barbella.

"Give examples of Rossian in *English!*" demanded Olaf Umea.

"Class—"

"I give honderd examples!" flashed Olga Tarnova. "Vodka! Caviar! Borscht!"

"Dose are foods, not woids!" gibed Mr. Kaplan.

"Borodin! Dostoevsky! Pushkin!"

"Zeez are *names!*" objected Christian Fledermann.

"All Rossian!"

"But dose woids *stay* Rossian!" exclaimed Mr. Kaplan.

168

"We want woids which pass into *English.* Kip your borscht an' blintzes, Tarnova! Push away Pushkin! *Homogenize* somting in Russian! Did Rossians give us a name for automobills? Talaphone? A hot drink? Iven a cold sneck?" Mr. Kaplan was waxing indignant.

"Mr. Kap—"

"You are prajudiced against Rossia!" railed Miss Tarnova.

"He'sa jalous Italia, too!" alleged Mr. Barbella.

"We must all be *broad*minded," cut in plaintive Miss Mitnick. "Mr. Kaplan, you are not international—"

"Ha! I didn't objact to Chinese tea!"

Mr. Parkhill was rapping his pointer so sternly, and frowning so frostily, that he stilled the factions by sheer force of will. "Nothing is to be gained by these heated exchanges! We are here to study, not argue." Stigmata of shame spread across the faces he beheld. "Since some of us seem to feel so intensely about this, I suggest that those who wish to—may bring to our next session a brief list of words, *English* words, which you recognize as—being of foreign origin!"

That was how it had begun. Just that simply. Who could have foreseen that Mr. Parkhill's suggestion would open the dikes to a flood?

For that was precisely the way Mr. Parkhill felt now—flooded, inundated by wave upon wave of words, names, roots, prefixes, suffixes, rolling across the room from distant and exotic shores. No sooner had he finished calling the roll than Lola Lopez, who must have consulted half the Spanish-speaking population of New York, rattled off words of Hispanic vintage, beginning with "arena," ending with "tobacco," and including four extrapolations of "cigar."

Miss Lopez had scarcely run out of breath before Miss

169

Atrakian, who seemed to have plundered her fiancé's knowledge of Homer and Euripides, began flinging gems from the Aegean before the barbarians. And no sooner had the dust settled in Miss Atrakian's path than Mr. Barbella was pouring out melodious syllables culled from the Tyrol to Calabria. And before his last, ringing echoes had expired in the fervent air, Olga Tarnova, bosom heaving, eyes smouldering with strictly retroactive love of Holy Russia (civilization had been throttled there in 1917, as far as Miss Tarnova was concerned), began to intone a Slavic litany.

Mr. Parkhill had never heard anything like this before. Christian Fledermann followed Miss Tarnova with proud loot from the Rhineland, ranging from "edelweiss" to "kindergarten" to "pumpernickel." Mr. Wodjik donated several vocables from some Balkan clime, which, since no one could understand them, joined the ranks of English without challenge. Mr. Nussbaum offered three words which bore the proud, albeit intermediary, *imprimatur* of Israel: "shlep," "kibitzer," "mish-mosh." To this, "Cookie" Kipnis, a fastidious spirit, added "bagel," which inspired the widow Pilpul to toss in "lox."

Mr. Wilkomirski, who often misunderstood an assignment, rose above the call of Poland to present words from three languages in which he had not the slightest vested interest: "carnival," "whiskey," "kimono." Even Oscar Trabish, fatigued from his work before the ovens, yawned, " 'Chef'. . .'menu'. . .'omelet'—all Franch!"

"Pistol!" cracked Mr. Hruska, tapping the Czech. To which Mr. Barbella, beside himself with piqued patriotism, flung " 'Bank'! 'Sofa'! 'Pepper'!" into the teeth of his colleagues.

The room was beginning to resemble the Olympic games.

Mr. Kaplan had remained surprisingly mute throughout

the etymological parade. Now he sought to catch Mr. Parkhill's attention. He did this with mooings, hummings and
"Psst! Psst!"'s which reinforced a beseeching expression
that implied he would die on the spot unless recognized.
It proved unnecessary for Mr. Parkhill to do so, because
Mr. Kaplan, divining the intent, anticipated the act. He
leaped to his feet, announced, "I have woids from all over
de seas!" and strode front and center.

All the other students had recited from their seats, of
course; but Hyman Kaplan was not the man to forfeit the
advantage of an erect speaker over a recumbent audience.

"Frands, fallow students, all-Amaricans!" Mr. Kaplan
paused. "I say 'all-Amaricans' because only in a school in
wonderful Amarica can we show soch pride in the conter-
butions from foreign nations! In this megnificent etmos-
phere—"

"Mr. Kaplan," Mr. Parkhill broke in, "this is *not* an exercise in Recitation and Speech. Simply present your
words."

"I shouldn't give beckground remocks?" Mr. Kaplan
might have been Apollo, asked to discard his lyre.

"No," said Mr. Parkhill stonily. "There is no need whatever for background—re *marks.* "

Mr. Kaplan hefted a piece of chalk with a sigh that wed-
ded injury to innocence, and printed nine letters on the
board:

EUMOIROUS

Spots floated before Mr. Parkhill's eyes.

"What?" That was outraged Olaf Umea.

"Is that a word or a disease?!" guffawed Mr. Nathan.

"Some people got a noive like gallstones!" That was Mrs.
Yanoff, heaving in black.

"What is the word?" Mr. Olansky asked frantically.
"What did he do to the board?"

"Mr. Kaplan," frowned Mr. Parkhill, "I—"

"He wrote 'humorous' with 'e-u'!" Miss Gidwitz informed Mr. Olansky.

"The woid is not 'humorous'; it's 'eumoirous,'" remarked Mr. Kaplan.

"Fake!" howled Mr. Olansky. "A fake word!"

"Watch this mon's treecks!" warned Miss Tarnova.

"Eumoi—' Oy?!" oyed Mrs. Moskowitz.

"Class . . ." Mr. Parkhill floundered in misery. In all his years as a teacher, no pupil had ever brought a word into the classroom which Mr. Parkhill could not explain; Mr. Kaplan had bagged a specimen Mr. Parkhill could not even recognize. His eyes bored into the nine letters on the blackboard. What an ungainly—an outlandish—word! A Grecian word (that was clear); but what a freak: Mr. Parkhill wondered whether any Greek had ever used it.

"Eumoirous . . . eumoirous. . . ." It raced through Mr. Parkhill's head. The prefix, of course, meant "good," and "moir"—from "moira"?—perhaps had something to do with destiny. "Euphorious!" popped into his mind. Could Mr. Kaplan possibly have meant "euphorious" instead of "eumoirous"? There was, after all, a good deal about Mr. Kaplan that was emphatically euphorious.

"Where *did* you get such a crazy word?" he heard Mr. Olansky roar.

Mr. Kaplan pointed a regal finger at the stand in the corner on which Webster's Dictionary reposed.

"Pssh!" Mr. Pinsky slapped his cheek, chortling.

Mr. Nussbaum clutched his beard and prayed.

"Mr. Kaplan," said Mr. Parkhill carefully, "suppose you tell us what that word—means."

"It's from Grik."

The laconic reply only fanned the wrath of the forum.

"Answer Mr. Parkhall!"

"Don't play pick-a-boo with the question!"

"This beats Barnum and Paley!" laughed Nathan P. Nathan.

"Mr. Kaplan," said Mr. Parkhill drily. "I do not doubt that your word is—or comes from—Greek. But that is not what I asked you. I asked: What does the word mean?"

"Don't *you* know?" asked Mr. Kaplan in astonishment.

Mr. Parkhill stared at the blackboard glumly. He would not dissemble; he would not evade. "No." The moment the irretrievable negative left his lips, Mr. Parkhill regretted it. The entire grade was staring at him—their teacher, their Solon, their Solomon—in horror. The very foundation of education was crumbling before their eyes.

"Teacher don't know a word?" Milas Wodjik was thunderstruck.

Tomas Wodjik asked the same question; but backward: "A *word* teacher don't know?"

"A foreigner can stump an American-born?" Miss Ziev was so aghast she fingered her engagement ring to remind herself that not all was lost.

"*Mr.* Parkhill . . ." Miss Mitnick, wan, bewildered, could say no more.

They were like passengers on a storm-tossed ship whose captain confesses a total ignorance of navigation.

"Class . . ." Mr. Parkhill adjusted his glasses, smoothed his tie, teetered back and forth on his heels, forced a vapid smile upon his lips—all the while fighting for time. "Let us not make mountains out of molehills. No one can know —or use—all the words in English. There are, after all, half a million words in the language"—a heart-rending *"Gewalt!"* came from Mrs. Moskowitz, whose nerves collapsed at the prospect of half a thousand—"and no one can possibly keep all of them in his head. That, in fact, is one of the reasons we have dictionaries! . . . Now, Mr. Kaplan, suppose we come directly to the point. Define 'eumoirous'!"

Strangely enough, Mr. Kaplan did not appear pleased. He did not even look contented. He looked flabbergasted, even apologetic, a Boswell who had accidentally sent Dr. Johnson sprawling in the dust.

Mr. Kaplan lifted a blue slip of paper from his pocket. Dolorously, he read: " 'Eumoirous. Adjective....' It means, says the dictionary, 'Happy'; also 'fortunate from good intantions or good actions.' " He lowered the blue slip contritely.

"Shame, shame on such word!" hissed Miss Tarnova.

"Crazy!" mumbled Mr. Hruska.

"*I* wouldn't make Mr. Parkhill such trouble!" announced Rochelle Goldberg through her lozenge.

"Give Koplan a diploma!" lashed out Mr. Olansky. "Greduate him! Now! Good-bye!"

"Good-by-y-ye!" echoed Olaf Umea.

Not a retort or riposte came from Hyman Kaplan. He stood in silence and (could such a thing be?) regret.

"Well, class," said Mr. Parkhill. "Mr. Kaplan has certainly brought us a—uh—most unusual word."

"That woid is not unusual; it is unbelievable!" bellowed Mr. Blattberg.

"For that blame Grik, not Keplen," said Mr. Kaplan.

This gambit so enraged Mr. Blattberg that he began swinging his watch chain as if it was the sling not of David but of Goliath, yearning to kill David with his grandsons' baby teeth.

"Kaplen, give an *inch,*" pleaded Bessie Shimmelfarb.

"Class!"

"You are not fair, Mr. Kaplan!" blurted Miss Mitnick, verging on tears. "Mr. Parkhill wanted words that would help, not confuse—"

"Som people," sighed Mr. Kaplan, "can drown in a gless of water."

"Now he gives swimming lessons!" raged Mrs. Pilpul.

"Gentle—"

"Everyone else in the class brought in useful words!" cried Miss Mitnick.

"Does aducation have to be useful?" rejoined Mr. Kaplan.

"In a hundred *years* we wouldn't use a word like 'eumoirous'!" Miss Mitnick wrung her hands in despair.

"Could come an occasion for *som* student in this room to use 'eumoirous,' " Mr. Kaplan murmured.

"Mr. Kap—"

"The day you use that cockamamy word," stormed Mr. Olansky, "snakes will fly and elephants sing!"

"Keplen," said the name's owner, "is not responsible for the animal kingdom."

"*Mr.* Kaplan!" Mr. Parkhill did not try to soften his annoyance. "I entirely agree with Miss Mitnick and Mr. Olansky! Your word is *most* obscure. Good English is simple English. The purpose of words is to communicate, not to impress. And a word such as 'eumoirous'—"

Mr. Kaplan's features sagged like wax in the sun. He had obviously expected Mr. Parkhill to praise him for discovering so exceptional a word as "eumoirous," perhaps even hold him up to the class as a model of ambition and courage. Instead, Galahad saw King Arthur leading the Saracens.

"Now let us proceed to dangling participles!" Mr. Parkhill picked up the textbook. "Page seventy-five . . . Mr. Kaplan, you—may return to your seat."

For the remainder of the evening, Mr. Kaplan sat silent, wrapped in desolation. The man had retired to the tent of hurt pride, and within it—who knew his thoughts? Only as the hour of departure drew nigh did Mr. Kaplan bestir himself—and then only to bend head over notebook and, without sound or sign, begin to write.

At long last, as Mr. Parkhill himself was becoming sated

with dangling participles, the final bell chimed its signal of adjournment.

The exhausted scholars collected their notebooks, stuffed their brief-bags and satchels, cleared the hook-slat of coats and hats and scarves, donned their garments, and streamed to the door.

"Good night, Mr. Parkhill."

"Good ivning."

"So lung."

"See you next time."

Mr. Parkhill returned the parting phrases as he sorted out his books and papers. He reached for his attendance record—and frowned. Mr. Kaplan was still in his seat, still writing. Mr. Parkhill made more noise than necessary in closing the desk drawer.

Mr. Kaplan rose. "Goot night," he said, pausing before Mr. Parkhill, then closed the door as he went out.

Mr. Parkhill sank into his chair. Rarely had he felt so tired. His neck was stiff. He leaned back, irritated anew by the squeaking of the chair's unoiled spring. He began to massage his temples.

He had harbored such high hopes for "words from foreign sources." He remembered an admirable article in *PARSE,* the journal for English teachers, some months ago, an article by Dr. Helmut Ganshmeier of M.I.T., titled "Cognates: Vital Clues from Foreign Tongues." . . . Dr. Ganshmeier was a linguistic wizard who had become so fascinated by word-roots in culture diffusion that he had moderated a symposium on "Psycho-Linguistics." What novel, what challenging ideas that issue of *PARSE* had contained. But Dr. Ganshmeier had never been forced to deal with a student like Hyman Kaplan. . . .

Mr. Parkhill rubbed his eyes. On the desk he saw a sheet of foolscap. It was folded. He reached over and unfolded the page. Something was written on it, but upside down. He turned it right side up.

Dear Mr. Parkhill—

Tonight I disagreed with you. Still you are the best teacher.

If I dont learn from you, I wont learn from anyone!

(singed)

Hyman Kaplan

p.s. You should feel eumoirous.

Mr. Parkhill tossed the paper on the desk with impatience. That was just like Mr. Kaplan—to find a way, however canny, however pertinacious, to prove his point, to have the last word whatever the ruse. . . . "Eumoirous . . . Happy from good intentions or actions."

Well, Mr. Parkhill told himself, he did not feel at *all* eumoirous!

He put on his hat and rubbers before a delayed awareness of incongruity made him pause. "(Singed) Hyman Kaplan." Why, Mr. Kaplan had spelled his name without stars!

Mr. Parkhill picked up the note again. It was true. "Hyman Kaplan" lay in gloomy black. Without crayoned colors. Without red letters outlined in blue. Not garnished with a single star of green.

Then a gleam of color caught his eye. On the underside of the fold, which he had not seen before, was printed:

TO MR. P*A*R*K*H*I*L*L

As he switched off the lights, Mr. Parkhill wondered whether he would ever again be so honored.

He felt eumoirous.

177

FOR THE BEST IN PAPERBACKS, LOOK FOR THE

In every corner of the world, on every subject under the sun, Penguin represents quality and variety – the very best in publishing today.

For complete information about books available from Penguin – including Pelicans, Puffins, Peregrines and Penguin Classics – and how to order them, write to us at the appropriate address below. Please note that for copyright reasons the selection of books varies from country to country.

In the United Kingdom: For a complete list of books available from Penguin in the U.K., please write to *Dept E.P., Penguin Books Ltd, Harmondsworth, Middlesex, UB7 0DA*

In the United States: For a complete list of books available from Penguin in the U.S., please write to *Dept BA, Penguin, 299 Murray Hill Parkway, East Rutherford, New Jersey 07073*

In Canada: For a complete list of books available from Penguin in Canada, please write to *Penguin Books Canada Ltd, 2801 John Street, Markham, Ontario L3R 1B4*

In Australia: For a complete list of books available from Penguin in Australia, please write to the *Marketing Department, Penguin Books Australia Ltd, P.O. Box 257, Ringwood, Victoria 3134*

In New Zealand: For a complete list of books available from Penguin in New Zealand, please write to the *Marketing Department, Penguin Books (NZ) Ltd, Private Bag, Takapuna, Auckland 9*

In India: For a complete list of books available from Penguin, please write to *Penguin Overseas Ltd, 706 Eros Apartments, 56 Nehru Place, New Delhi, 110019*

In Holland: For a complete list of books available from Penguin in Holland, please write to *Penguin Books Nederland B.V., Postbus 195, NL–1380AD Weesp, Netherlands*

In Germany: For a complete list of books available from Penguin, please write to *Penguin Books Ltd, Friedrichstrasse 10 – 12, D–6000 Frankfurt Main 1, Federal Republic of Germany*

In Spain: For a complete list of books available from Penguin in Spain, please write to *Longman Penguin España, Calle San Nicolas 15, E–28013 Madrid, Spain*

FOR THE BEST IN PAPERBACKS, LOOK FOR THE

PENGUIN BESTSELLERS

Cat Chaser Elmore Leonard

'*Cat Chaser* really moves' – *The New York Times Book Review*. 'Elmore Leonard gets so much mileage out of his plot that just when you think one is cruising to a stop, it picks up speed for a few more twists and turns' – *Washington Post*.

Men and Angels Mary Gordon

A rich, astonishing novel of the limits of human and divine love.' A domestic drama of morals with a horrifying climax . . . compellingly readable' – *Sunday Times*. 'A brilliant study of the insatiable demands of the unlovable' – *Standard*

The Mosquito Coast Paul Theroux

Detesting twentieth century America, Allie Fox takes his family to live in the Honduran jungle. 'Imagine the Swiss Family Robinson gone mad, and you will have some idea of what is in store . . . Theroux's best novel yet' – *Sunday Times* (Now a powerful film.)

The King's Garden Fanny Deschamps

In a story which ranges from the opulent corruption of Louis XV's court to the storms and dangers of life on the high seas, Jeanne pursues her happiness and the goal of true love with all the determination and his spirits of one born to succeed . . .

Let No Man Divide Elizabeth Kary

Set against the turmoil of the American Civil War, *Let No Man Divide* tells of Leigh Pemberton's desire to nurse the wounded and live an independent life, and her secret yearning for Hayes Bannister, the man who has saved her life and taken her breath away.

Is That It? Bob Geldof with Paul Vallely

The autobiography of one of today's most controversial figures. 'He has become a folk hero whom politicians cannot afford to ignore. And he has shown that simple moral outrage can be a force for good' – *Daily Telegraph*. 'It's terrific . . . everyone over thirteen should read it' – *Standard*

Niccolò Rising Dorothy Dunnett

The first of a new series of historical novels by the author of the world-famous *Lymond* series. Adventure, high romance and the dangerous glitter of fifteenth-century Europe abound in this magnificent story of the House of Charetty and the disarming, mysterious genius who exploits all its members.

The World, the Flesh and the Devil Reay Tannahill

'A bewitching blend of history and passion. A MUST' – *Daily Mail*. A superb novel in a great tradition. 'Excellent' – *The Times*

Perfume: The Story of a Murderer Patrick Süskind

It was after his first murder that Grenouille knew he was a genius. He was to become the greatest perfumer of all time, for he possessed the power to distil the very essence of love itself. 'Witty, stylish and ferociously absorbing . . . menace conveyed with all the power of the writer's elegant unease' – *Observer*

The Old Devils Kingsley Amis

Winner of the 1986 Booker Prize
'Vintage Kingsley Amis, 50 per cent pure alcohol with splashes of sad savagery' – *The Times*. The highly comic novel about Alun Weaver and his wife's return to their Celtic roots. 'Crackling with marvellous Taff comedy . . . this is probably Mr Amis's best book since *Lucky Jim*' – *Guardian*

FOR THE BEST IN PAPERBACKS, LOOK FOR THE

PENGUIN BESTSELLERS

Goodbye Soldier Spike Milligan

The final volume of his war memoirs in which we find Spike in Italy, in civvies and in love with a beautiful ballerina. 'Desperately funny, vivid, vulgar' – *Sunday Times*

The Nudists Guy Bellamy

Simon Venables, honeymooning under the scorching sun, has just seen the woman he should have married . . . 'It is rare for a book to be comic, happy and readable all at once, but Guy Bellamy's *The Nudists* is just that' – *Daily Telegraph*. 'Funny caustic and gloriously readable' – *London Standard*

I, Tina Tina Turner with Kurt Loder

'Tina Turner . . . has achieved the impossible; not one but two legends in her own lifetime' – *Cosmopolitan*. *I, Tina* tells the astonishing story that lies behind her success; electrifying, moving and unforgettable, it is one of the great life stories in rock-music history.

A Dark-Adapted Eye Barbara Vine

Writing as Barbara Vine, Ruth Rendell has created a labyrinthine journey into the heart of the Hillyard family, living in the respectable middle-class countryside after the Second World War. 'Barbara Vine has the kind of near-Victorian narrative drive that compels a reader to go on turning the pages' – Julian Symons in the *Sunday Times*

Survive! John Man

Jan Little, with her husband and daughter, escaped to the depths of the Brazilian jungle. Only she survived. Almost blind and totally alone, Jan Little triumphed over death, horror and desolation. Hers is a story of remarkable courage and tenacity.

A Man Made to Measure Elaine Crowley

Set in Dublin during the First World War, the story of *A Man Made to Measure* follows the fortunes of a group of people whose lives are changed forever by the fateful events of the Easter Uprising. 'Elaine Crowley writes like a dream . . . an exciting new discovery' – *Annabel*

FOR THE BEST IN PAPERBACKS, LOOK FOR THE

PENGUIN OMNIBUSES

Life with Jeeves   P. G. Wodehouse

Containing *Right Ho, Jeeves*, *The Inimitable Jeeves* and *Very Good, Jeeves!*, this is a delicious collection of vintage Wodehouse in which the old master lures us, once again, into the evergreen world of Bertie Wooster, his terrifying Aunt Agatha, and, of course, the inimitable Jeeves.

Perfick! Perfick!   H. E. Bates

The adventures of the irrepressible Larkin family, in four novels: *The Darling Buds of May*, *A Breath of French Air*, *When the Green Woods Laugh* and *Oh! To Be in England*.

The Best of Modern Humour   Edited by Mordecai Richler

Packed between the covers of this book is the teeming genius of modern humour's foremost exponents from both sides of the Atlantic – and for every conceivable taste. Here is everyone from Tom Wolfe, S. J. Perelman, John Mortimer, Alan Coren, Woody Allen, John Berger and Fran Lebowitz to P. G. Wodehouse, James Thurber and Evelyn Waugh.

Enderby   Anthony Burgess

'These three novels are the richest and most verbally dazzling comedies Burgess has written' – *Listener*. Containing the three volumes *Inside Enderby*, *Enderby Outside* and *The Clockwork Treatment*.

Vintage Thurber: Vol. One   James Thurber

A selection of his best writings and drawings, this *grand-cru* volume includes *Let Your Mind Alone*, *My World and Welcome to It*, *Fables for Our Time*, *Famous Poems Illustrated*, *Men, Women and Dogs*, *The Beast in Me* and *Thurber Country* – as well as much, much more.

Vintage Thurber: Vol. Two   James Thurber

'Without question America's foremost humorist' – *The Times Literary Supplement*. In this volume, where vintage piles upon vintage, are *The Middle-aged Man on the Flying Trapeze*, *The Last Flower*, *My Life and Hard Times*, *The Owl in the Attic*, *The Seal in the Bedroom* and *The Thurber Carnival*.

FOR THE BEST IN PAPERBACKS, LOOK FOR THE

PENGUIN OMNIBUSES

The Penguin Book of Ghost Stories

An anthology to set the spine tingling, including stories by Zola, Kleist, Sir Walter Scott, M. R. James and A. S. Byatt.

The Penguin Book of Horror Stories

Including stories by Maupassant, Poe, Gautier, Conan Doyle, L. P. Hartley and Ray Bradbury, in a selection of the most horrifying horror from the eighteenth century to the present day.

The Penguin Complete Sherlock Holmes   Sir Arthur Conan Doyle

With the fifty-six classic short stories, plays *A Study in Scarlet*, *The Sign of Four*, *The Hound of the Baskervilles* and *The Valley of Fear*, this volume is a must for any fan of Baker Street's most famous resident.

Victorian Villainies

Fraud, murder, political intrigue and horror are the ingredients of these four Victorian thrillers, selected by Hugh Greene and Graham Greene.

Maigret and the Ghost   Georges Simenon

Three stories by the writer who blends, *par excellence*, the light and the shadow, cynicism and compassion. This volume contains *Maigret and the Hotel Majestic*, *Three Beds in Manhattan* and, the title story, *Maigret and the Ghost*.

The Julian Symons Omnibus

Three novels of cynical humour and cliff-hanging suspense: *The Man Who Killed Himself*, *The Man Whose Dreams Came True* and *The Man Who Lost His Wife*. 'Exciting and compulsively readable' – *Observer*

FOR THE BEST IN PAPERBACKS, LOOK FOR THE

PENGUIN CLASSICS

John Aubrey	**Brief Lives**
Francis Bacon	**The Essays**
James Boswell	**The Life of Johnson**
Sir Thomas Browne	**The Major Works**
John Bunyan	**The Pilgrim's Progress**
Edmund Burke	**Reflections on the Revolution in France**
Thomas de Quincey	**Confessions of an English Opium Eater**
	Recollections of the Lakes and the Lake Poets
Daniel Defoe	**A Journal of the Plague Year**
	Moll Flanders
	Robinson Crusoe
	Roxana
	A Tour Through the Whole Island of Great Britain
Henry Fielding	**Jonathan Wild**
	Joseph Andrews
	The History of Tom Jones
Oliver Goldsmith	**The Vicar of Wakefield**
William Hazlitt	**Selected Writings**
Thomas Hobbes	**Leviathan**
Samuel Johnson/	**A Journey to the Western Islands of**
James Boswell	**Scotland/The Journal of a Tour to the**
	Hebrides
Charles Lamb	**Selected Prose**
Samuel Richardson	**Clarissa**
	Pamela
Adam Smith	**The Wealth of Nations**
Tobias Smollet	**Humphry Clinker**
Richard Steele and	Selections from the **Tatler** and the **Spectator**
Joseph Addison	
Laurence Sterne	**The Life and Opinions of Tristram Shandy, Gentleman**
	A Sentimental Journey Through France and Italy
Jonathan Swift	**Gulliver's Travels**
Dorothy and William Wordsworth	**Home at Grasmere**